I0685506

A Sunrise Kind of Love

Love in Sunrise Series Book 1

Loran Adelle Davis

L.A. DAVIS BOOKS

eBooks cannot be sold, shared or given away as it is an infringement on the copyright of this work.

This book is a work of fiction. The names, characters, places, and incidents are products of the writer's imagination or have been used fictitiously. Any resemblances to persons, living or dead, events, locales, or organizations are coincidental.

A Sunrise Kind of Love
© 2021 Loran Adelle Davis
LA Davis Books

Editor: Bethany Hendrix
Cover: Alistair Cameron
Logo and Designs: Alistair Cameron
Images from: Stock Photo Secrets

All Rights Are Reserved.
No part of this book may be used or reproduced in any manner without the prior written permission of the copyright owner, except for the use of brief quotations in a book review.

First Edition: June 30, 2021

Check out my website and sign up for my newsletter for updates!

Description

Makiya

I always dreamed this day would happen. The day where Hunter would show up on my doorstep and confess his undying love for me. I never stopped loving him no matter how hard I tried, no matter how angry I was at him for leaving.

Now, after five long years of waiting, he leans against my car with the same cocky smirk he wore when we were younger. Damn, if my body doesn't react to him as if there was never any time lost between us. Just his gaze roving over my body makes me feel tingly all over.

I hate how smug he looks like he knows how he still affects me. I hate that my heart still wants him after everything he's done.

What I hate most of all, though, is that he's about to find out the secret I've been keeping from him all these years. And he's going to be pissed.

This is going to change my life forever.

Hunter

Secrets? Really, that's how we're playing this game? We're keeping secrets from each other. The Ki I knew would have never kept something this big from me, but I guess she isn't the same girl I knew.

I'm not the same guy either. She thinks I don't want anything to do with her. That's why she kept this from me. Well, she's about to find out the cold, hard truth.

I'm not leaving without a fight, and I'm definitely not giving her a chance to walk away from me this time.

I spent too many years of my life, hiding from my love for her. It's about damn time for me to stop running. So, Ki better get used to the fact that she's going to see my handsome face everywhere.

Challenge accepted.

Contents

To all those too terrified to chase your dreams.
Don't let the fear win. Reach out, take those dreams, and make them
everything you ever wanted and more.
Much love to you all!

One

Makiya

"Ki, what the heck are you doing? Get off your ass and come help me," my best friend yells from across the café.

"This is a public establishment Sabrina, you can't say ass in here," I holler back, laughter in my voice.

"Okay, boss lady, then why did you just say it?" She pushes back her long dark hair, allowing me to see the smug look on her face.

"Because I'm the boss. I can do whatever the hell I want to," I say, winking at her, before turning back to my coffee at hand. "Besides, it's my break."

"Oh, so we get breaks now?"

I pick up a napkin laying on the table, ball it up, and toss it as hard as I can in the direction of the counter, avoiding several people currently waiting in line. The laughter on their faces tells me they're enjoying what's going on as much as I am.

Good, it's what you ask for when you visit a small-town café.

The customers laugh even harder when the napkin ball lands about twenty feet away from the counter and nowhere near Sabrina.

"And that's why I was always better at softball than you," Sabrina states with a quick smirk in my direction.

I stick my tongue out at her. "You're just jealous."

She laughs so hard she almost chokes and several of our customers do the same. I'm glad to see everyone thinks I'm hilarious.

"Of what?" she manages to blurt out between snorts of laughter.

"My witty, intelligent, sassy personality. Oh, and let's not forget my unfathomable beauty." I cross my arms in front of me and tilt my head to the side, daring her to argue with me.

I knew she wouldn't though, even if she disagreed with whatever I said. It's one of the beautiful things about Sabrina - her loyalty to friends and her undying belief that kindness makes the world go round.

She snorts, "Whatever you say, boss."

I laugh as everything in my mom's quaint, little coffee shop slips back to normal. I continue to sip on my dark roast coffee and listen to the soft voices that surround me as customers catch up on the gossip of the week.

It's one of my favorite things about working in my mom's café. Though, I guess it's mine now, even if it still feels weird to call it that. To me, it's always been my mom's coffee shop.

The decorations remind me of her every time I look at them. Bright blues and yellows mixed with silver and white shine throughout the café. She was a bright woman, just like the colors she chose. She'd always said she wanted the café to represent her.

And it had.

Even now, two years after her passing, as I watch the people walk by on their morning commute, the café remains the same. The sweet aromas of freshly baked pastries and the sound of the soft country music still hang in the air.

I inhale a deep breath, noting the subtle hints of coffee and breakfast sandwiches that settle around me. As the only place to get good coffee and breakfast food in Sunrise, the Sunrise Café prides itself on being one of those places that always makes you feel at home.

Which is why we include the free shows for our customers. I smirk into my coffee.

I've always felt at home here, soaking in the sounds of children and adults laughing and talking about their days or the smell of my personal creations coming from the oven in the back.

That might be partly because I've spent every waking minute in this place since I was old enough to walk.

Mrs. Cransky, an older lady I've known most of my life walks up to my little table. "You know, dear, the only reason I come here every morning is to watch you and Sabrina battle it out."

I chuckle. "Oh really?"

"Of course, it's better than any of those daytime soaps. You two go at it like an old married couple." Her eyes widen and her mouth forms an "O." "You're not…?"

I assume she means a lesbian, but I'm not really sure. "Together? No, Mrs. Cransky, I like men way too much."

She winks at me. "Me too, deary, the bigger the better I always say."

"At this point, size doesn't really matter to me as long as the sex is good."

Mrs. Cransky waves me off with her hand while she laughs at me. "See, this is what I mean? Way better than TV," she mutters as she walks away.

Like I say, we pride ourselves on making our customers feel at home.

I finish the last bit of coffee and stand. Picking up my empty cup, I carry it into the washroom and place it in the dishwasher. I hear giggling coming from the back room and smile.

My precious baby girl peers around the corner, beckoning me with her hands to come to the backroom. "Momma," she squeals, "Grandpa is being silly again."

I laugh freely.

My father didn't know how not to be silly. All my life he'd been telling "dad" jokes like they were going out of style. It was one of those things I loved the most about my father. That, and his gentle way with people.

I walk back towards her and peek around the corner of the office door where I see my father sitting with a brown paper bag over his head and speaking with a French accent. "Do zey sell baguettes here?"

"Really, dad? You're supposed to be working." The look of this giant of a man with a paper bag on his head has me laughing once again.

He pulls the bag off his head and pretends to pout. "Hannah, this was supposed to be our little secret," he says, his chocolate eyes, so much like mine, giving him away with a twinkle.

Hannah giggles and hides her mouth behind her hands. "Sorry, Grandpa," she says, her big green eyes peering over her fingers.

She makes it so hard to be angry at her, just like her father. I know it has to do with the eyes. There is just something about those big green eyes that make her seem so innocent.

Well, that, and the fact that the love I have for my little girl far outweighs any anger I ever feel towards her.

I push Hannah's dad from my thoughts and look towards my Dad. "I can't do all this by myself, Dad."

"I know. I know, Ki. I'm working on it. Just keep the customers happy, and I'll get the paperwork together." He points his hand toward the doorway, back toward the kitchen.

I grab my daughter by the shoulders and guide her towards the door. "Come on, baby, you can help Momma whip up some more pastries."

"Yessss!" she squeals, running towards the kitchen.

I swear squealing is her main mode of communication.

I look back at my father who now stares intently at the papers.

For a brief minute, I see my mom sitting there in his place with a pencil behind her ear and her fingers between her lips as she bites her nails.

God, I miss her so much.

My mom morphs back into my father, and I have to pull myself away from the door before my dad sees the tear sliding down my cheek.

Normally, I'm not this emotional when I think about my mom, but this café was my mom's dream. She made it become the booming center of town.

I remember working here as a kid, doing exactly what Hannah does: standing next to my mom and making new batches of pastries as the front counters emptied out.

I smile at the memories.

I can't believe it's been two years since she lost her fight to cancer. I wish she could see this place again. I bet she'd be so proud of how well it's doing.

"Mommmmmmm," Hannah yells from the kitchen, breaking my thoughts.

I pull myself back together, brushing the few tears that escaped away as I enter the kitchen. Hannah has her favorite pink apron wrapped around her waist and is standing on her stool next to the counter. "Someone is a little excited to start baking."

She gives me a big grin. "This is my favorite part about Saturdays."

"Mine too, sweet girl." I give her a side hug, then reach for my own apron.

We begin the process of mixing the ingredients together and forming the pastries. My hands move without instruction, with only the sounds of bustling customers out front playing in my ears.

"Mom, can I ask you something?" Hannah looks to me, her brows furrowing as she speaks.

My heart skips a beat as Hunter's face pops into my head, but I quickly shove it aside, ignoring the way my hands bead with sweat. I swipe my hands across the bleach white apron hanging from my neck. She's never asked *that* question. But I have an open door policy with my daughter. All questions allowed no matter how much I may dread answering them.

"Sure, baby, you can ask me anything," I respond, feeling my gut churn.

"Where's my daddy?"

I fumble with the egg in my hands as she asks *the* question – the one that makes my heart race and my breath catch in my throat.

A piece of the shell falls into the bowl, and I mutter a string of curse words under my breath. I battle with the eggshell, eventually winning and tossing it into the trash. Once I do, I turn to Hannah, her green eyes piercing my heart.

She looks just like her father, and she knows it. My golden hair is no match for her fiery red locks and her green eyes look nothing like my milk chocolate ones. She is her father through and through.

Damn Hunter and his good genes.

I don't know how to answer her question.

I'd known Hunter my whole life. We grew up in the same small town, merely blocks away from each other. Sunrise was simple like that, a private tourist town along the coast of South Carolina that prided itself on staying true to its roots with not a stoplight to its name.

The beauty of its simplicity is that as kids we were allowed to wander the streets all day. Hunter and I met when we were 8 years old and became fast friends. I even pulled my best friend Sabrina into our crew.

But senior year was when things changed between us. Hunter noticed me, like really noticed me, for the first time. He wanted me, and I couldn't resist his football captain charm.

It wasn't until after Hunter had already left for college that I found out I was pregnant. When I went to tell him the news, I found him in bed with some blond bimbo. I couldn't blame him - he was at college, and I was still in Sunrise, so I backed out then. I couldn't burden him with a baby. But how do I tell my five-year-old daughter that I chickened out?

I can't.

Not because it will hurt her, but because she won't understand.

For a brief moment, I wonder where the question came from. Then, I remember Hannah is learning about families at school, which makes me clench my fists tight.

I know she's in Kindergarten, and it's a natural part of education for a five-year-old, but I wish desperately that she hadn't learned about the "ideal" family. It makes me feel like a really shitty person.

I try to compose myself while I come up with a string of lines that could potentially satisfy her question. Finally, I speak, "Look, Hannah, your daddy..." I pause.

Kill me now.

I don't know how to do this.

I hear a soft voice float through my head. *Be honest with her, Ki. She deserves to know the truth.*

It's from one of the last conversations I had with my mom. I cried as I told her about my fear of someday having to tell Hannah about her father. My mom, always wise and very blunt, told me to just tell her the truth.

What is the truth though? I barely even know.

I close my mind and take a deep breath.

I can do this.

I just have to be honest.

"Hannah, your daddy was a good man, but he had big dreams, so he couldn't be here with you the way he wanted to."

Sure, that isn't the entire truth, but it *is* pretty damn close. At least, it sounds good to me.

Hannah takes in my words. Her mouth moves back and forth showing me what I already know. She's thinking about what I said, and knowing my daughter, she doesn't like my answer.

Finally, she asks, "Momma, does my daddy love me?"

I swear I can't catch a break.

How the hell am I supposed to answer *that* question?

I don't know if he loves her because he doesn't even know about her. I mean, I'm sure he would love her, but I can't tell her that. I love my baby girl more than life itself, but right now, I want to scream out my frustrations.

I count to ten, calming myself down before responding.

Here goes nothing. "Hannah, your daddy and I haven't talked in a very long time, but I'm sure that he loves you more than life itself."

"How do you know, Momma?"

"Because that's how much I love you." I whisk her into my arms and squeeze her tight.

She is my everything. I did what I had to do to protect her. I have to remind myself of that.

"I love you too, Mom."

I kiss her pale cheek and whisper in her ear. "Come on, let's get to work on these pastries. We don't want our customers to go hungry." She giggles in my ear and my heart slows down again. Just like we never had the conversation at all.

I stick the last of the dishes in the sink. Mario, my dishwasher, smiles at me as I give him more work to do. He's an older man with salt and pepper hair, but his age doesn't keep him from staying fit. His muscles work as he cleans the pots and pans that I had just laid by the sink. He always tells me that he loves when I'm baking because he knows he'll always have a job.

"Ki, I need you out here," Sabrina yells from the front register, sounding flustered.

"Be there in a second," I holler back.

Reaching for Hannah, I wrap her in my arms. "I need to go out and help Sabrina. Do you want to go sit with Grandpa?"

Hannah shakes her head at me. "No, Momma, I want to help you."

I can't help but smile at her stubbornness. She might have Hunter's green eyes and his bright red hair, but she has my heart and soul. "Come on, let's go."

We walk out to the front of the café, and I smile at the number of people sitting and standing around drinking their tea or coffee.

My mom would be so proud right now if she could see how good business is for us. She always believed this place would succeed. She just didn't have a chance to see it all the way through.

I push back the lump in my throat as I approach the counter, Hannah by my side.

An older lady standing by the counter waves at us. "Hello, Mrs. Berkley." I greet her with my best smile.

"Mrs. B, what do you have for me today?" Hannah shrieks, jumping up and down.

Mrs. Berkley laughs softly, making her eyes crinkle around the sides. A widow of about fifty, Mrs. Berkley is one of a kind. When my mom passed, she took Hannah under her wings and treated her as her own.

Every Saturday, she brings her some kind of book or toy that she picked up shopping that week. As much as it hurts sometimes knowing my mom isn't here, I am so grateful Hannah has Mrs. Berkley.

I love how much the people in this town care for us, especially after my mom died. This town had pulled together and made sure that Dad, Hannah, and I were all okay. That's one of the many reasons I never want to leave this place.

Mrs. Berkley lifts a bag up so Hannah can see it. "Come give me a hug, squirt, so you can have your present."

Hannah pulls her hand from mine and flies around the counter. Once she reaches Mrs. B (as she calls her), she jumps into her arms, squeezing tight. She leans her head back to look at Mrs. Berkley. "Mrs. B, I love you." She speaks quietly as if it is a secret.

Mrs. Berkley smiles back. "I love you too, squirt."

Two

Hunter

I stand in line at the Sunrise Café, reveling in how many hours I spent here growing up. The town looks exactly the same as it did when I left for school five years ago.

Just as small.

Just as suffocating.

The buildings haven't changed much on Main Street, a few additions here and there to the signs and businesses, but that's it. There are still no stoplights, parking lots, or chain restaurants.

Honestly, I don't even know why I'm here.

I step forward as the line in front of me moves. I've never seen the café this busy before, but I'm glad it is. Most of the tables are full of friends or families chatting away. The entrance to the store, where I'm currently standing, has people packed together either waiting on their orders or waiting to place one.

A rough hand lands on my shoulder, and I cringe as a booming voice rings in my ear. "Is that Hunter? Big college football star?"

Come on, not now.

I turn to the man that I neither know nor care about and simply smile at him.

This is the reason I never come home to visit. Everyone always wants to relive my past, something I have no desire to do.

Not after what happened last year.

The perks of being a football star in a small Southern town. I may not know them, but they all sure as hell know me.

Turning back to the counter, I catch a glimpse of the real reason I decided to brave the Sunrise Café and all its customers this morning. Her golden hair cascades down her back and her brown eyes shine with happiness. A little girl bounces beside her happily. Probably a customer's child excited about the pastries.

My heart jumps as memories of the two of us together pop into my head, and I pull the reins back in.

Not going to happen.

She's probably married by now anyway, and if she isn't, I'm sure she doesn't want me anymore.

I finally reach the counter and place my order.

Sabrina's eyes bulge as she registers who I am. "Hunter? What on God's green Earth are you doing here?" She sounds surprised, maybe a little afraid, as her head swivels to where Ki disappeared into the back.

I'm confused as hell by the tortured look on her face, but I ignore it.

"It's good to see you too, Sabrina," I respond. She hands me my change and tells me to have a seat. I take the seat closest to the counter, hoping I might get another glimpse of my past.

As I sit, I contemplate Sabrina's reaction. It was weird, obviously, but I have no idea what I did to cause *that* response.

We'd been friends back in the day. In fact, it had always been me, Makiya, and Sabrina. We grew up in the same neighborhood just a few houses down from each other. Things between the three of us changed once I stopped looking at Ki like she was my friend and started wanting her in so many different ways.

Sabrina and I weren't as close after that - maybe that was why she had acted so weird.

I shake off the gnawing sense that something isn't right as Sabrina places a mocha in front of me. To some, a mocha may be too girly, but at least I wasn't drinking a chai tea or some shit like that.

She turns to leave, but instead, she stops and sits down in the chair across from me.

"Hunter, you shouldn't be here."

"And why the hell not, Sabrina? This is a public place."

"Maybe so, but you know who owns this *public place*." She glares at me.

What the hell is her problem?

"Ki doesn't need this," she continues. "She doesn't need to see you, not after what you did."

Well, now I know why she was acting so weird.

I left Makiya and she's pissed at me for that. I can't blame her; Ki is her best friend. I understand her defending Ki but telling me I can't be here is a bit ridiculous. I have no excuse for what I did back then, but hell if I'm going to be told I can't get coffee from the only café in town.

"Look, just because Ki's mom owns this place, doesn't mean I can't be here. I mean this is public property." I argue, knowing it won't fly with Sabrina. She loves Ki too much to take my bullshit. Not to mention, she'd always been able to see right through me.

Her face drops at my words. *Shit, what did I say?*

"No, Hunter, Ki's mom doesn't own this place. Ki does. Sally passed away two years ago from cancer."

Damn, I had no idea. Why didn't my parents tell me? I mean it's not like we hadn't talked every week for the last five years. In fact, my mom and I had a standing phone date every Sunday. Why wouldn't she mention something this big to me? "I'm sorry, Sabrina. I didn't know."

"I know you didn't. Ki asked your parents not to tell you. She didn't want you coming back here during your last year of football."

My heart aches at her words.

Even after I left her with no word, she had protected my dream.

Little does she know that it hadn't mattered anyway.

I screwed it all up on my own.

I suck in a deep breath, trying to control the emotions flowing through me.

Anger.

Fear.

Regret.

And maybe a little love.

"I should have been here," I say.

Sabrina shakes her head at me. "No, Ki wanted it this way. Hunter, you hurt her. You left her."

I want to argue with Sabrina. I didn't have a choice; I had to leave for football.

But I can't because I know she's right.

I didn't have to leave the way I did. I chose to leave without a word or a goodbye because I thought it would be easier for me. I was a selfish bastard and never, for one second, thought about how much I would hurt Ki.

"I didn't mean to hurt her," I plead with Sabrina to understand.

She reaches for my hand, a simple gesture between old friends. "Hunter, she went to see you. She found you with some blonde between your legs. You didn't just hurt her; you ripped her heart out." She pats my hand and stands.

Turning back to me, she states simply, "It would be better if you weren't here."

I tap my fingers on the table in front of me. I don't really agree with her, but I concede anyway. "I'll leave, Sabrina. For what it's worth, I really am sorry."

"You're a little late for sorry, Hunter," she says as she walks away from me. I drain the last of my coffee and make my way to the door.

Stepping out into the warm southern air, I take in a deep breath.

I'm an idiot.

It's the only thing I can think to say to myself. I thought I came back here for my brother's wedding, but maybe I had come back for an entirely different reason - to make things right between Ki and me.

I reach my truck parked in the lot on the side of the café. I know I should leave, but something stops me.

I see her car parked behind the café, that same Honda she had in high school. I smile at the thought of her standing next to it, looking up at me with those big brown eyes.

God, I didn't have a clue what I let go back then.

I shake her image out of my head and look at my watch: one o'clock. The café will close in an hour.

I move my feet towards her car and lean against it. I don't know why I have the sudden urge to see her, but I do. Might as well get it over with now.

Three

Makiya

I wipe the sweat from my brow as I lock the door and flip the sign to closed. Thank God we don't stay open past two on Saturdays. I'm exhausted.

The one good thing about owning this place is that I can make the hours. We are closed tomorrow, and I am in desperate need of a day off.

I make my way back to the kitchen, shutting off the lights as I go. Even though my staff has already done it once, I check after them to make sure everything is turned off, specifically the oven. My slightly obsessive nature won't let me leave until I make sure there is no chance of an accident.

I continue checking behind my employees as I make my way to the back room. It's not that I don't trust my employees to do their jobs correctly, but this place means too much to me to not be extra careful.

Hannah sits with her tablet in front of her playing some games. My dad left about an hour ago and offered to take Hannah with him, but she insisted she wanted to stay with me. "Hannah bear, it's time to go."

"Okay, Momma." She hands me her tablet and scoots off the chair behind my dad's desk. She reaches for my hand, and I squeeze it tight as we walk out the back door.

"So, lovebug, what do you want to do this afternoon?" I ask her as I lock the door, but she doesn't respond.

I look down at her, but she stares at something off in the distance. "Hannah," I say as I follow her eyes.

I see the bulging arms covered in tattoos first.

I trail my eyes up until they see the hint of red stubble across his jawline and finally make eye contact with his piercing green gaze.

My breath catches as I realize who's standing in front of me.

For the love of biscuits and gravy, please no.

It can't be him.

"Momma, who is that?" Hannah points to the man I can't seem to take my eyes off.

My heart skips a beat and my stomach twists into nervous knots. Damn him for making me react the same way, even five years later. How can my body still feel like this around him?

I ignore my traitorous body and bring my attention back to Hannah's question. I pull her closer to me as I say, "He's no one, baby."

"Then, why is he standin' next to our car?" she asks.

She's too smart for her own good - or maybe mine - I can't decide. I'm too flustered by the reality of what's happening right in front of me.

"I don't know, Hannah, but we are going to find out." As we move closer to the car, my nerves pitter patter away and anger takes over. The past washes through me and fires me up.

Who the hell does he think he is, standing there looking all hot and sexy?

"Makiya." He mutters, a tinge of anger to his voice.

"Hunter," I mumble, avoiding eye contact. "What are you doing here?"

"I came for my brother's weddin'."

"I didn't mean in town, Hunter. I know your brother's getting married, we're invited. I meant what are you doing *here*," I say, pointing a finger at my car.

"I stopped by to see you earlier. Sabrina told me about your mom. The question I had, though, was why you didn't tell me."

I feel a tug on my hand. "Mom, how does he know Grandma?"

I stoop down to her level. "Hannah, can you please get in the car for me?"

"But mama," she whines, pulling on my arm and jutting her bottom lip out at me.

Seriously? There's no denying she's my daughter when she does that.

"Hannah," I say, my voice harsher than usual. Her bottom lip whimpers but she does as I ask with the whisper of "Yes, ma'am," floating on the air.

I reach in the driver's side and start the car for her. Then, I turn back to Hunter. "I didn't tell you because you left me Hunter. In case you hadn't noticed, we haven't talked at all in the last five years."

He just stares at me. "I know, and I'm sorry about that. I should have done things differently."

I huff at him. "Ya think? You didn't even say goodbye. I never heard from you again. That wasn't the plan."

"I thought it would be easier for both of us if we skipped the goodbyes."

Both of us?

Excuse me.

I know why he did it, and it wasn't to make it easier for me. He did it because he hates when people are upset.

He did it for himself.

Ugh, he is so selfish.

I feel rage seep through my veins, and I try to calm myself down.

With gritted teeth, I respond, "Well you were wrong, Hunter. Nothing about any type of goodbye is easy whether you say it to each other or not."

He nods his head and looks to the car where Hannah is, then back to me. "Ki, how old is Hannah?"

I look away from him as I try to control my breathing.

The moment I had dreaded all these years was finally here, and I don't have any freakin' clue what to do.

"Makiya." His voice is deep as he says my full name. He stares at me head on like a bull ramping up for a fight.

I give in, knowing he won't let it go if I don't. "She's five years old."

He nods, a look I can't quite read on his face. "She has my eyes," he states.

"She has your hair, too." I confirm what I know he's thinking – that's his daughter.

His eyes meet mine, and I see a depth of sadness. "Why didn't you tell me?"

A tear forces its way from my eye.

I don't want to do this. I don't want to have this conversation because if I do, I'll have to relive the past. But, right now, I don't have much of a choice. If anything, Hunter is persistent. He won't leave this alone until he gets what he wants.

I sigh softly. "I tried. I drove all the way to your campus when I found out. I asked around for your dorm room for an hour before someone gave it to me. I walked up to the door and found it unlocked. When I stepped inside, I heard the moans, your name on her lips. When I saw you with some blonde bimbo, I ran."

"Ki," he reaches for me, and I back away.

No, he doesn't get to touch me. Not after making me say that.

"Hunter, please don't. Whatever you're gonna say just forget it. I wanted to tell you about Hannah, but when I saw you with that girl, I knew you didn't care about me. How could you be with her if you did? I came home, told my parents I was pregnant and did it all without you." I reach for the door handle that Hunter leans against.

He moves, and I open the door. "Ki, I want to be a part of her life."

And there they are, the words I never wanted to hear.

What am I supposed to do now? Hell if I know.

Instead of responding, I climb in the car and squeal away from the parking lot as quickly as I can before Hunter has a chance to say anything else.

Five Years Ago

I can't believe graduation is only a month away. I've never been so ready for something in my life, even if it means not seeing my best friends as much anymore.

For once, I get to set out on my own and figure out what I really want in life.

My parents aren't too thrilled about that, especially my mom, but I know she'll be okay. I keep telling her we can talk every day, but she tells me it just isn't the same.

I curl the last strand of hair on my head, then brush the ringlets out with my fingers. The curls bounce back into place just around my chest.

I check my phone for the time and finish getting ready as quickly as possible.

One thing I've always loved about Hunter is how he's always on time, which can also be a little frustrating, especially when you're running late like I am now.

"Makiya Jane, your ride is here," my mom yells from the bottom of the stairs.

I ask her all the time why she insists on calling me by my full name when everyone else just calls me Ki. She simply tells me it's because she can.

I hate that response. It's a cop-out if you ask me like she doesn't really want me to know why.

I grab my phone off the bed and slide it into my back pocket as I rush down the stairs.

I swing the door open before I've even fully stepped off the bottom step – the beauty of the stairs being right behind the front door.

"Hey, Hunter!" I say, taking in his strong build and handsome face. A blush creeps up to my cheeks, and I mentally shake it off.

Gosh, when did I become the girl that has a crush on her best friend?

Once upon a time, he was a gangly teenager with an acne filled face, but somewhere in the last two years, his form became stronger and his face cleared up.

That's when things really started to change - when a simple touch or hug between best friends became an electric shock that I felt somewhere in the depths of my core.

"Be careful tonight, Makiya Jane, and remember, we love you," Mom's words break through my thoughts.

"Love you too!" I holler back, stepping outside and pulling the door shut behind me.

"Are you ready?" Hunter asks from beside me.

"Hell yea," I squeal back. "I'm always ready for a party.

He chuckles, pushing me forward with the gentle touch of his palm to my back. "I'm well aware," he says, referring to the party a few months back where I may have indulged a little too much and he may have had to carry me back to my house.

Not my proudest moment, but it felt good to have his arms around me.

I climb up into his rusty old hand-me-down truck and prepare for a night of much needed fun.

Four

Hunter

I stand there watching Ki pull away. I have a daughter.

Daughter.

I still can't believe it.

I have a daughter who looks just like me. How the hell did I not know that?

As Ki's car disappears, I walk back to my truck.

Climbing in, I start the engine and crank the music up, trying to drown out my thoughts. It doesn't work, though, and I find myself thinking about my daughter again.

Hannah.

At least, I think that was her name. It's what Ki had called her just minutes ago.

I want to know what she's like.

Clearly, she looks just like me, but is her personality more like her mother?

I laugh to myself softly. I know the answer to that without even talking to Hannah. Just the way she jutted her lip out at her mom when she asked her to climb in the car tells me everything. Ki always hated when she was left out or didn't get her way. I'd seen her do that exact same thing countless times growing up, and I'd also heard her say yes ma'am and do it anyway because that's how things are done in the South.

I pull my truck into my parents' driveway, staring at my childhood home. Nothing changes in this town no matter how long I'm gone. I climb out of my truck and grab my bag from the passenger side on the way down.

I let myself into the house as if I still live here and hear the familiar sound of pots and pans clanging from the kitchen.

"Mom," I yell, heading towards the noise.

"Hunter? Is that you?" she calls back.

She beams as I peer around the doorway. "Sure is."

She drops what she's doing and pulls me into a hug. "I'm so glad you're here. I've missed you so much. If you ever leave town for that long again, I swear I will hunt you down and bring you back myself."

I laugh at her. "Gee thanks, Mom, you always make me feel so loved."

She pats my cheek as she leans back to get a better look at me. "You know I will always love you."

"Yea, I do." I say, lovingly. I may not have been home over the last five years, but Mom always called to check in on me, make sure I was doing okay. Now Dad, on the other hand, we haven't had much contact over the years. We've never been real close. I think it has a lot to do with our different ideas about my life – he wanted me to work for his company, and I had no desire to.

I take a seat at the table and watch her get back to cooking. "What are you making?"

"Chicken 'n' dumplings."

"Yes!" I punch the air. Chicken 'n' dumplings are my favorite, and my mom always makes the best.

She smiles, and then opens and closes her mouth a few times like she wants to say something but doesn't know if she should.

Finally, she speaks, "I hope you don't mind, but I usually take some over to Ki's house when I make them."

I nod in understanding.

Wait a minute, does she know about Hannah?

If she does, I'm going to be really pissed that my own mother didn't tell me I had a daughter, especially since she had plenty of chances too.

I offer to take the food over to Ki's to see her reaction.

"I'm not so sure that's a good idea, Hunter. I mean Ki doesn't talk much about you, but I think there is still some bad blood between you two." My mom continues to stir the pot of dumplings as she responds to my offer.

I don't miss how she pretends to not know much about Ki or the way she avoids looking at me as she talks.

"I stopped by the café on my way over here," I blurt out.

She stops stirring the dumplings and turns to look at me, her mouth open in shock. She quickly gets herself back under control. "I wondered if you had. I knew it shouldn't have taken you that long to get here." She avoids making eye contact with me as she speaks.

"Did you know, Mom?" I ask, even though I already know the answer.

How can she not know?

She nods her head, and finally looks me directly in the eye. "I was with her the day she went to tell you. I was one of the first people she told besides her parents. She asked me to drive her down to campus since I knew where it was. I waited in the car as she asked around to see if anyone knew what building and room you were in since you hadn't told your father and I anything about it. You insisted on doing it all on your own.

"Anyway, when she figured out where the building was, I watched her walk inside, and then I watched as she came running out of the building with tears falling down her face moments later. I held her as she cried on my shoulder because she had walked in on something she didn't mean to. So, yes, I knew all of it."

I hear what my mom says, but my anger takes over. I ball my fist up on the table in front of me, prepared to hit anything I can.

I had every right to know.

Forget this.

Why did everyone in this damn town keep something this big from me?

"Why, Mom?" I question through gritted teeth.

"Hunter, you were in a bad place when you left here. I don't know why, and it's not my business; but you had always needed your freedom. You needed a chance to find yourself. I mean, it says enough that you haven't even come back to visit for the last five years, doesn't it? Ki didn't need to be hoping you might show up one day, and Hannah didn't need to wonder where her father was all the time."

"Was anyone ever going to tell me?" I growl in frustration.

All of this is unbelievable.

Wasn't I supposed to be the one to make the decision about being a father? Why did everyone feel it necessary to make that decision for me, especially my mom?

Surely, I could have made that choice on my own. I was eighteen. All I wanted was out of this God forsaken town but that didn't mean I wouldn't do anything for Ki.

But I had been afraid I would end up like every other damn person in this town. This life wasn't what I wanted.

That's what I had thought at eighteen anyway. I didn't want to be my parents and every other couple in Sunrise. I had wanted to be my own person, to live my best life. That had been why I ran in the first place.

I shake my head, too many thoughts running through my mind, almost missing my mom's soft response to my earlier question, "I was waiting until the right time."

"When exactly was that going to be?" I pound my fist onto the table, making my mom flinch.

She crosses her arms in front of her, a defense mechanism I'd seen plenty of times. "When my beloved son finally decided that it was time for him to come home. Until then, we had no intentions of telling you."

"Seriously?" I ask, my voice harsh. I know I shouldn't yell, but I also know that I can only see red right now.

"Yes, Hunter, because you may not care about anyone other than yourself, but I do. Both of them deserved better than this." My mom's words whip me harder than any belt I'd ever received as a kid.

I don't know why the words sting so much.

Maybe because she's right.

Five

Makiya

"I'm coming," I yell at the door as the bell continues to ring. Goodness gracious, don't they know it takes longer than five seconds for me to reach the door.

As I yank the door open, my mouth drops.

You've got to be kidding me.

What on earth is happening?

His smirk and the bowl in his hand tell me all I need to know.

"Are you going to let me in? Or make me stand outside all day?" he asks.

"I think I'll let you stand outside," I say, slamming the door in his face. He can't be serious. Does he think that I'm letting him anywhere near me and my daughter?

The doorbell rings again. I ignore it and walk back to the kitchen. My dad pops his head out from the living room. "Who the hell keeps ringin' the doorbell?" he yells from behind me.

"No one, Dad. Just ignore it," I tell him.

"Pretty damn hard to do when it's louder than my TV," my dad grumbles.

I walk around the island in our kitchen and continue chopping the vegetables for some stew. Dad has been begging me to make Mom's stew for the last week, and I finally have the time to do it. After five minutes of listening to the doorbell ring incessantly, it finally stops. I take a deep breath in relief and keep working on the stew.

As I place the last pile of vegetables in the pot, there's a knock on the kitchen door. I look to see who it is and roll my eyes. He has nothing to do with me for five years, but now, he won't leave me alone.

I walk to the door and pull it open. "Good grief, Hunter, can't you take a damn hint."

He gives me a crooked grin. "Mom made chicken and dumplings. She said she always brings you over some when she does. I offered to be the delivery boy."

My eyes open wide, and I speak before I get control of my thoughts. "And she let you?" I blurt.

He looks confused at my statement. Then, a sparkle of mischief twinkles in his green eyes. "Not exactly." I cross my arms in front of me and eye him with my best "mom" stare. He looks away from me as he says, "I may have stolen the container labeled for Ki and brought it to you without her realizing."

I almost laugh at him.

Almost.

All of this is completely ridiculous, but I don't crack a smile because it'll only encourage him. "Hunter, you shouldn't have come."

He eyes me curiously. "Do you mean come to your house or come to town?"

"Both," I state, crossing my arms in front of me. What does he think? That we can just pick up where we left off five years ago? No way is that happening.

"Ki, she's my daughter too, and I want to know her."

Damn, I want to argue with him. I want to say to hell with all of this. If he wants to know her so bad, he shouldn't have left. But I can't say any of that because this is my fault, too, and I know that. I should have told him even if I was pissed off that he was already sleeping with another girl. I could try to justify my actions a million times over, but I know I was wrong.

"What about when your brother's wedding is over, and you go back to wherever it is you've been for the last five years?" I ask him, getting to what's really bothering me. He should know our daughter, but I can't let that happen if he's just going to leave again.

"I don't have anything back there, Ki. I lost it all. I work a crappy job with great pay, but that's it. I was too ashamed to come home and admit failure, that's why I've stayed away." This time I do laugh. He's kidding me, right? Does he really think I'm going to believe this nonsense?

"You were ashamed? Of what?" I ask with major attitude. What does the amazing, small town superstar possibly have to be ashamed of, other than the fact that he ditched his family for football?

Hunter looks at me with solemn eyes. "You mean you don't know?"

"Know what, Hunter?"

"My senior year of college I blew out my knee in practice and had to have two surgeries. They said that even when my knee healed, I wouldn't be able to play football again. Another injury could leave me worse off than before. So, I finished my degree and got a crappy ass job. The big, bad football star destroyed his career because he was trying to show off."

I snort at his comment, trying hard not to laugh. "Gee, I can't imagine the big, bad Hunter trying to show off," I mock. It probably gives him the wrong idea, but I can't help myself. He always had a big head, even when we were kids. Showing off is just who he is.

A cocky smile spreads across his face. "You know I love it when you sass me."

My body shakes with something I can't quite explain.

Lust.

Attraction.

For the love of Pete, why do I still react to him?

 Mentally shaking it off, I respond, "Actually, no, I forgot."

"Mhm, I'm sure," he says smugly, like he knows what I'm feeling.

We stare at each other for a long minute, and every part of me wants to reach out and hold him again. I thought I didn't need Hunter. I thought that I was over him, but the minute I saw him I knew that I wasn't.

Not even close.

And that scares the hell out of me. If he could leave me once, he could leave me again. How can I trust him to stay this time? How can I trust him not to hurt Hannah?

I can't.

I need to remember that.

"Momma," Hannah yells from the hallway leading to the kitchen. My eyes grow wide. Any minute she'll bust into the kitchen, and she'll want to know why this man is here again. "You need to go now, Hunter."

"I want to meet her, Ki. She's my daughter, too," he pleads.

"Not now, Hunter, please. I can't take that chance. I need time to figure all of this out." I walk towards the back door and open it for him.

He just stands there, staring at the door. I can see the anger in his eyes. I can practically hear the debate that must be going on inside his head, trying to convince himself what's right and wrong.

Finally, he takes a step towards the door. Before he walks out, he whispers, "This isn't over, Ki. I'll prove myself to you, anyway I have to."

"Good luck," I respond with a smirk as I shut the door. I turn to see Hannah standing in the doorway of the kitchen.

"Mom, why was that man here again?" she asks with her eyes scrunched together in confusion.

Damn. She moves swiftly and silently, doesn't she?

"He was just bringing over Mimi's chicken and dumplings," I smile softly. "You want to help me finish the stew? After, we can decide which meal to eat for dinner."

"Sure," she says as she twirls around the island, the matter settled.

For now.

"Momma, dinner was so yummy tonight," Hannah compliments me as she slides out of her chair. She carries her bowl to the sink like I taught her to do.

Dad sits next to me, staring into his bowl. He'd looked at me curiously when he came in for dinner and saw the dumplings laying out. I know he wanted to say something, but Hannah was with me, so he didn't.

I brace myself for his questions as Hannah excuses herself to the playroom.

"Makiya Jane Carter, are you going to tell me what that boy was doing here today or am I going to have to call his mom?" Oh dear, this is going to be a rough conversation.

"Dad, I'm not in high school anymore."

"Sure could've fooled me with the whole sneakin' 'round behind my back," he grumbles as he takes another sip of soup.

I roll my eyes, just like I'd done so many times in high school. "Seriously, Dad? I was sneakin' 'round because of Hannah, not you."

He places his spoon in his bowl and looks up to meet my gaze. "Why would you need to be sneakin' 'round because of Hannah?"

"Hunter is back in town. He stopped by the café this afternoon without me knowing. Found him waiting outside my car when we went to leave."

"So, he knows about Hannah then?" Dad asks, rubbing his forehead with his hands.

It isn't like he's the one who should be stressed out. I'm the one who should be freaking out.

"Kind of hard to keep it a secret. She looks just like him. Not to mention, he's smart enough to do math, Dad," I respond sarcastically.

I know my dad doesn't mean it like that, but I'm confused enough.

"Ki, ditch the attitude and sarcasm for a minute. This is serious business," he demands as I stand from the table.

I pick up my bowl and reach for his. "You done?"

He nods his head.

I put both our bowls in the sink then grab two beers from the fridge. I place one down in front of my dad.

Sitting back down, I pop the lid off my beer and take a sip.

"I don't know what to do, Dad. He wants to meet Hannah officially, but I don't know if he's serious or thinks this could be a fun game of house until he's ready to leave again." I take another sip and sit my drink back down.

I'm not one to ask my dad for help, but he's all I have left.

"So, what did you say?"

"I told him not yet, that he needed to prove to me he meant what he was saying."

My dad's face is contemplative as he mulls over my words. I imagine him thinking about what my mom would say if she were here. I figured she would say something along the lines of, "Screw him. He lost his chance."

I laugh to myself at the thought. That was the kind of person my mom was – no nonsense, no second chances, and stubborn as hell.

In a way, I'm a lot like my mom, but I have so much more of my dad in me.

He stays silent a few minutes longer, probably thinking over his words.

We're the same that way.

We think everything through before we speak or act.

My mom, she wasn't like that. She said how she felt with no regrets.

Sometimes, I wish I could do that, but I'm so afraid to hurt people.

Finally, Dad speaks, "I'd like to think your mom would agree with what I'm about to say, but I know she wouldn't. All I can do is give you advice from my point of view as a man and a father. I know he hurt you, and I hate him for that, but he's her father. He deserves the chance to get to know her. I can only imagine how he feels right now, but I know it can't be good."

I suck in my dad's words, thinking about each and every one of them.

He's right.

His words make perfect sense, but that doesn't stop fear from coursing through my veins.

Could I give him a second chance? *Would* I give him a second chance? Did he really deserve one after everything?

Deep down, I know he does and that makes everything so much more terrifying.

Six

Hunter

I close my parent's front door behind me as softly as I can, hoping to get away with my surprise trip to Ki's house. I slip my shoes off and gently put my keys on the keyring. Turning, I jump.

"What the hell?" I scream as my eyes focus on my mom standing in front of me, her hands folded across her chest and her eyes glaring at me through tiny slits.

"Hunter James Hart, have I taught you nothing?"

Shit, she's pissed. I can see it in her eyes, but the anger in her voice is far worse.

"I told you not to go to Ki's, but you did it anyway. What on God's green earth were you thinking?"

Anger rushes through my veins at her words.

"I was thinking that everyone in my life lied to me and I wanted to get to know my daughter!" I yell at my mom.

Her face softens as my words hit her. She sighs, the anger draining out of her. "I'm sorry, Hunter. We didn't do it to hurt you. We did it to help you."

I know she means what she says, but I can't figure out how it helped me. From where I stand, it only hurt me more.

"Well, if you could tell me how the hell it helped, that'd be great. 'Cause right now all I feel is anger and hurt because I missed out on five years of my daughter's life." I respond, pushing past my mom into the kitchen. I need a stiff drink, but beer will have to do.

When I shut the fridge, I look up to see my mom pulling out a chair at the table. She stares at me for a long moment before opening her mouth. "Hunter, please sit."

I do as she asks, sitting opposite her at the old oak table.

"You've always had a wild 'n' free soul. As a kid, you only ever wanted to play football and fish. You had such a talent for football, too. And I was so happy to support you because I knew you were going to do great things with it. When you got the full ride to play in college, I never doubted you'd take it. I was so proud of you for it, but I also knew you needed it. You were never happy in this small town. The way you talked about your future I could tell." She pauses for a minute to wipe away a tear.

"You were my baby, but you needed your chance to shine. When Ki told me about the baby, I knew you'd want to know so I helped her. We drove up there that day with no clue that she would find what she did. When she came out to the car crying and told me what she'd seen, I knew you weren't ready yet. You hadn't had your chance to be free, to experience life the way you needed to. I never wanted to lie to you, but it's what you needed at the time." Mom reaches for my hand, grasping it between her two.

Everything she says makes sense, but it doesn't make the hurt go away.

My mother had lied to me.

Lied.

For five years.

Every time I had called to check in, she never once said a thing about my daughter.

Even though I'm pissed that no one told me, a part of me understands.

"What do you think I should do Mom?"

"About what?"

"I want to know my daughter, but Ki isn't too keen on that at the moment. How do I make her see that I'm serious?" I ask genuinely.

I want to know my daughter, desperately. I may not have made the best decisions in my life, but that doesn't mean I'd turn my back on my child.

Mom smiles at me and squeezes my hand between hers. "Just be there for her, Hunter. It's all she ever wanted from you."

Be there for her? I've only had to worry about myself for the last five years.

I can do it though, right?

If it's the only way I can get to know my daughter, then I know I'll do anything I have to. I just have to figure out how to do *that.*

"Do you have her number?" It's a stupid question. I know my mom has her number - I should have asked if she'd give me her number.

My mom looks at me, wearily. "Depends on what you're planning to do with it."

"Be there for her, Mom. She doesn't want me to meet Hannah yet, which means she doesn't want me around. How else am I supposed to be there for her?" I ask, because hell if I know.

I'm not proud to admit it because my mama raised me better than that, but I can't help the fear that overtakes me when I think about commitment. I have avoided it at all costs most of my life until Ki.

My parents have been happily married for almost thirty years, but they never did anything with their lives besides have kids. My dad went to work for his dad at the construction company, and my mom stayed at home with us.

And there's nothing wrong with that life. It just wasn't the life I had seen for myself, but now, as I sit here with my mom, I start to rethink all of it.

The dream I had ditched Ki for failed epically thanks to me.

The things I always said I didn't want ended up being what I got.

Maybe it was time to reevaluate everything.

"Actions speak louder than words, Hunter, just remember that," Mom's voice breaks through my thoughts. She lets go of my hand, grabs a piece of paper, and writes something on it.

I hope its Ki's phone number, but I'm not sure I'm that lucky.

She hands it to me as she says, "Whatever you do, don't screw this up."

Well I'll be damned. It *is* Ki's number. She must be feeling awful bad about lying to me now; that's the only way to explain her giving me this number.

She stands from the table, then stops. Looking over her shoulder, she points at me. "You did not get that number from me, ya hear?"

I salute her and laugh, "Yes, ma'am."

She shakes her head as she leaves the kitchen, but I stay at the table debating whether or not to text Ki.

It's close to nine by now and knowing Ki, she's already snuggled into bed.

Even when we were kids, she had always gone to bed early. Sabrina and I had made fun of her for it in high school, but she always said she was just a morning person.

Once, when we were fifteen, she had told me that the reason she went to bed so early was so that she could be awake for the sunrise.

Of course, I told her she was crazy. No sane person woke up that early just to watch the sunrise. She had just laughed at me and told me not to knock it 'til I tried it.

The next night, I snuck over to her house and climbed in through the bedroom window like I'd done so many times over the years. I slept on the floor, and when her alarm went off the next morning, I climbed out on the little overhang outside her window along with her.

We sat there watching the sun come up, just like we'd sat together so many times watching it set. She looked at me with those gorgeous eyes of hers that made me feel so at home, and said, "The sunrise is the start of a new day. It reminds me that, even in our darkest moments, there is always a fresh start waiting; a new beginning of sorts."

I hadn't known what to say to her at the time, but the memory hits hard now. I had just lived through some of the darkest times of my life.

Maybe coming back to Sunrise was my second chance.

My fresh start.

My new beginning.

Aw hell, I'm starting to sound like a chick.

Seven

Makiya

After the longest and most emotional day I've had since my mom died, I finally lay down in my bed. I grab my blanket and burrow myself in the soft, plush throw.

Who needs a man when you have the warmth and softness of an amazing blanket to snuggle with?

Not me, that's for sure.

Everything that happened today has me so confused. My thoughts are all twisted up and so is my stomach. I haven't felt this anxious since before I started taking my anxiety medication.

I try to calm the thoughts racing through my mind with some deep breaths, but it doesn't help. How the hell am I going to sleep with thoughts of Hunter running around inside my head?

I hadn't thought about him in a long time. I'd finally accepted the fact that I would never see him again. Then, there he was just waiting by my car, then at my front door, and then again at my back door.

Damn, he was persistent - And as much as I hate him for it, I also understand why.

I *had* kept the biggest secret from him.

Buzz. Buzz.

I pick up my phone to check my messages. A picture of Hannah and I makes up the background of the screen that lights up with a text from an unknown number.

I click on the text and read:

Hey Ki, it's me, Hunter. I just wanted you to know that I'm here for good.

I laugh out loud as I read his message.

He's here for good?

Not likely.

He seems to forget that I know him better than anyone else, and I know if he left me once, he could do it again.

I throw my phone down on the bed and roll over so that I face the ceiling.

But what if he does mean what he says?

What if he really is ready for us? Then again, what if he isn't?

I keep saying this is all because of Hannah, and part of it is, but it's also about me.

Last time, the heartbreak was unbearable. I can't go through that again.

I take a few deep breaths again, trying to relax my mind.

I reach for my phone, opening my messages. I save his number, and then I type:

Good night, Hunter.

Then my mind wanders to a time that seems so long ago now.

Five Years Ago

I lean my head back against the rear window of Hunter's truck and stare out at the sunrise coming up over the low country.

It's so peaceful and quiet. The only sounds around us are the chirps of insects and lapping water.

I pull the blanket up over my shoulders and stretch out a little further in the back of the truck. Hunter leans in closer to me and wraps his arm around me, pulling me in tight.

A contented sigh falls from my lips. "I'm going to miss this," I whisper.

"Me too," Hunter mumbles.

I can't ignore the feeling that washes over me as I sit curled up by his side or the heat that pulls within my belly at the thought of him holding me as we watch the sun make its ascent into another day. And I can't deny the desire for him to kiss me that fills my soul.

I feel like one of those pathetic, love-struck girls. Hell, maybe I am, but I don't want to be.

I just can't help it. I feel so much more aware of the crackles between us, the bolts of fire and electricity that spark when we're together.

Sabrina tells me not to do anything about it – that he'll just hurt me, but I don't believe her.

I know Hunter. I know he's sweet and caring. And, most importantly, I know he'd never hurt me. He couldn't.

I find myself relaxing deeper into him as my thoughts carry me away into daydreams of me and him – a couple.

Eight
Makiya

Morning comes way too early, and with it the sound of my alarm buzzing in my ear. I roll over, opening my eyes just wide enough to turn off the alarm set for 4 AM.

That's the worst part about owning a coffee shop: the crazy early morning hours.

I may be a morning person, but not *this* early of a morning person.

I get out of bed and start my morning routine. My dad always watches Hannah for me while I open so she's one less thing I have to worry about in the morning. Plus, she'd never forgive me if I woke her up at 4 in the morning.

As I put the finishing touches on my makeup, my phone buzzes from across the room.

I walk over, pick it up, and read the name attached to the messages.

Great.

Hunter.

A couple days have passed since we'd first seen each other, but every morning he texts me, and every morning, I don't respond.

I'm really not ready to deal with this.

Whatever *this* is.

I have too much going on and not enough mental capacity.

His mother had called me the day after he showed up to apologize for giving him my number and to express her thoughts on the situation. I value her opinion more than anyone's. She's been there for me for all of it, but he is also her son. I knew the minute she began talking that she thought Hunter was ready.

I'm still not convinced.

In fact, he has a whole lot more convincing to do.

I read the good morning message and lay my phone back down on the nightstand. I finish getting ready, then head to the coffee shop. As I pull into the parking lot, I almost forget to put the car in park when I realize whose truck is in the lot and who stands outside my cafe.

Seriously?

What the hell is he doing here?

I jump out of my car - thankfully remembering to put the car in park - and walk over to him, anger radiating off of me. My nostrils flare and my face scrunches together, my fists clench tightly by my side. Somehow, I get out the words, "What are you doin' here?"

Hunter stands with his arms crossed and a smirk on his handsome face. "I'm here to help."

"You don't work here," I remind him as I push past him to unlock the door.

"No, but you do, and usually alone. I thought ya might like some help," he explains, shrugging his shoulders.

I want to smack that smug look off his face. I don't need any help from the man who tore me to pieces.

"I wanted help five years ago when I found out I was pregnant, but, ya know, shit happened. I don't want your help now," I say firmly, walking through the back door to the shop. I move so fast that I forget to make sure the door shuts before Hunter can come through.

Great.

I turn and there he stands with that annoying smirk on his face.

Looking deliciously handsome.

I throw my bag down on the desk and reach for my apron, wrapping it around my waist.

I cannot think about Hunter in that way. He's not mine.

Not anymore.

"Come on, Ki, you might not want my help, but you need it," he insists, taking up the entire doorway of the back office.

"I don't need anything from you Hunter. I've been doin' just fine without you in case you hadn't noticed," I yell at him in frustration.

He's only making me want to punch him even harder right now.

Does he honestly think I need him? Surely, he's joking. Obviously, he forgot who he's talking to.

I push past him towards the kitchen, and I hear his footsteps following behind me. I swirl around on my heels, nearly slamming my face into his hard, defined chest.

I forgot how much I love his muscles.

He puts his hands up in defense. "Okay, poor choice of words. I admit it."

"Ya think?" I screech as I turn back to the counter, reach for the dough I had laid out the night before, and then preheat the oven.

Silence fills the space as I continue with the morning routine before we open. I know he can tell I'm angry. Each of my movements are hard and there may be some slamming of bowls and pans going on.

He doesn't say anything though, and neither do I.

He just continues to stand there, watching me and not moving.

As I knead the dough and stir the icing, I feel myself grow calmer and more levelheaded. Baking is a release for me, one release I really need right now. I let myself go through the motions and feel the peace settle around me.

After a good thirty minutes, my annoyance has lessened, but he still stands there, watching me. If he isn't planning on leaving, I may as well put him to work. "You really want to help?"

A grin forms on his face. "So, you do need me after all?"

"No, I don't need you, but I also don't need an audience. So, if you insist on standin' there watchin' me, you may as well help." I throw a pair of oven mitts at him as the timer on the oven goes off.

There.

Now, let's see how he does in the kitchen. I guarantee he'll be begging *me* for help in no time.

I admit that when I first saw Hunter standing outside my shop, I was furious. Now, as I watch him work his way around the kitchen, I'm glad he's here. He's turned out to be slightly more helpful than I first thought.

I'll never tell *him* that, though.

Sabrina called in sick this morning and everyone seemed to choose today to want coffee and pastries. Not that I'm complaining; we need the business.

I turn back to the customer in front of me, handing them their bag of pastries and coffee, and I smile as they leave the café.

I hear heavy footsteps coming from behind me just before he speaks, "Finally, some peace and quiet. Is it always this busy in here?"

I laugh at his appearance. His hair sticks up in several places, flour clings to his black shirt, and sweat drips down his neck.

How does he still manage to look so good when he's such a mess?

"Not usually," I respond, "but business has picked up a lot lately."

Hunter leans against the doorframe that separates the kitchen from the front and crosses his arms over his chest, making him look even sexier than I remember. "I suppose that's a good thing, but you must be exhausted."

"Yes, it's a good thing, but you're totally right. It's exhausting," I agree as I sit down in a chair at the table next to the register, trying my hardest not to look at him.

At this point, there's only one patron left in the shop: a younger man working on his laptop. He's a regular who comes in for one cup of coffee at 11 and stays until we close at 2 almost every day. I don't complain, though, because business is business, and he keeps to himself.

"So," Hunter pauses, breaking me from my thoughts and forcing me to look at him, "what are your plans for later?"

I lean back against the chair and cross my legs in front of me. "What do you mean?" I ask.

"Like what are you doing this evening?"

What am I doing this evening?

The same thing I do every Wednesday.

I'll pick Hannah up from school and take her to soccer practice. Spring soccer season started not too long ago. She's pretty good for being five, and she loves playing.

Then, we'll head home, eat dinner, and get ready for the next day. But Hunter doesn't need to know all that.

"Not much," I finally answer, looking away again.

He nods his head as he pushes off the door frame. He knows I'm lying. I can see it in his eyes.

He takes the seat across from me at the table. "Why do I get the feeling that isn't exactly true?"

I sigh at his question. "What do you want me to tell you, Hunter?"

"Preferably, the truth," he snorts.

The truth?

He doesn't really want the truth because the truth is that he isn't going to get to see Hannah.

Not tonight at least.

"You want the truth? Okay, I still don't trust you, and I still don't think it's a good idea for you to meet Hannah. So, no, I am not going to tell you what I'm doing tonight because it's not your business."

He frowns, stands from the table, and heads back to the kitchen. As he reaches the doorway, he glances back at me. "If that's how you feel, then I guess I'll have to change your mind."

Change my mind?

I'd love to see him try.

Nine

Hunter

I know I shouldn't be here sitting in my jacked up black Chevy, debating whether or not to get out to watch my daughter at soccer practice. I know Ki doesn't want me here. That part's obvious by the fact that she refused to tell me about it earlier. But I couldn't *not* come.

When I had left the coffee shop, I got home to find my mom on the phone with Ki talking about Hannah's soccer practice tonight. I didn't even think as I got in my truck and drove over here, I had to come, even if Ki will be pissed at me when she sees me.

But, I can't seem to get out of my truck. As tough as I may seem, what, with the tattoos and clothes, I'm not nearly as tough as I look.

Not when it comes to Makiya.

She's probably the only person in the world, besides my parents, that absolutely terrifies me.

She knows me better than anyone, which also means she knows my weaknesses and exactly how to gut me without the help of a knife.

So, I decide to watch from my truck a little longer.

Spring in Sunrise, South Carolina was always my favorite. Not too hot, not too cold – it was just the right temperature with a mixture of equally sunny and rainy days, unlike the bleak winters and brutally hot summers.

I catch sight of Hannah's bright red hair flying behind her as she runs down the field. She chases the ball closer and closer to the net. As she reaches the net, she kicks the soccer ball as hard as her little legs can manage and it soars straight inside. She stops in her tracks and glances back at Ki who is bouncing up and down from excitement.

How can she think I don't want this?

I want more than anything to be standing next to her while our daughter plays her heart out on the field.

I should be celebrating the goal our daughter just made! But she took that option away from me when she chose not to tell me.

I shake my head. *Not this again.*

I can't keep going over everything I missed out on and everything I should be doing with my daughter now. Shit happened. Ki is partly to blame for it, but so am I and I'm man enough to admit that.

Mom told me to be there for her and I'm determined to do just that. I reach for the handle of my truck and swing open the door. I don't care if Ki doesn't want me here. I'm here, and I won't let her force me to leave.

As I slam the door shut with a mixture of nerves and rage, Ki turns to look at me. The emotions I feel are expressed all over her face with a tight smile forming wrinkles across her forehead. I move towards her as fast as I can, giving her little time to think.

"Hey, Ki," I greet her as I stop just short of the blue camping chair that she has set out behind her.

"What are you doing here?" she growls at me.

That's a question she seems to be asking me a lot lately, and one that I don't really have an answer to.

The fierce look in her eyes isn't lost on me. If I were being honest, I'd probably admit that it turned me on a little to see her like this.

"Heard Mom talking to you about the practice. Thought I might come take a look." I shrug my shoulders as I step closer to her. I stop next to the chair, this time only a few inches away from Ki. "She looks great out there."

Ki's face relaxes into a wistful smile. "Yea, she loves the game. She's good, too." She continues to watch our daughter play.

Our daughter.

The thought still shakes me to the core and fills me with a sense of rage and amazement I can't quite describe. I don't think it'll ever make sense in my mind, but there's no going back now that I know about her.

Together in silence, we watch Hannah play until practice is over. Ki looks to me, worrying her lips between her front teeth. "She's going to want to know why you're here, but I won't tell her the truth."

I nod my head.

I understand.

I do.

I hurt her, but she's hurting me every minute she keeps me from knowing my daughter.

I can't stop the way my fists ball up or the way my arms and shoulders tense at the ever-present anger within me lately.

I want to lash out at her, but I don't. Not here. She deserves better from me. I need to listen to my mom's advice and trust that Ki will let me know Hannah in time. I just need to prove to her I'm not going anywhere.

"I'll see you tomorrow, Ki." I move to leave, even though I don't want to go without seeing Hannah.

"Why?" she asks abruptly, stopping me.

I circle back around to face her, noticing the distance that now separates us. Her brows are scrunched together. I know why she's confused. "I need something to do, and you seem to need my help at the shop."

I know those words irritate her. I can see her hands fly straight to her hips and her lips turn into a frown. "I don't need your help, Hunter. I have an employee." So she keeps telling me, but that won't stop me.

"And?" I counter as I turn to head to my truck.

"Fine," she shouts behind me, "But you better not be late."

She knows I'll be there. I'm not a liar like *some* people I know. But I really need to stop letting my thoughts drift back there. I can't make things work the way I want to if I don't let this shit go.

I know Ki wants to hate me, and I feel the same way. But whatever we had as kids is still there. No amount of anger can change the way she makes me feel.

Five Years Ago

"Dude, when did Ki grow those things? She's looking fucking hot today!" Asher says beside me, punching my arm to get my attention.

I move my eyes to where he's looking and see her – my best friend. And, holy fuck, is he right.

She's always been gorgeous, but damn, the outfit she's wearing today accentuates every single curve. My hands itch to walk over there and touch her, but it wouldn't be anything like the friendly touch we're used to.

I fight the urge and force my eyes away from her, landing on Asher's face which is still glued on Ki.

"Earth to Asher," I growl, snapping my fingers in front of his face and fighting the impulse to knock him out for staring at my girl.

My girl? *She's not my girl. She can't be. She means way too much to me for me to change things between us.*

I'll just fuck it up anyway like I always do.

I haven't had one serious relationship in the last four years. The girls are always too clingy or too demanding or too, well, whatever.

But, if I'm being honest with myself, the biggest problem is that they aren't Ki. They can't hold my attention like she does or make me laugh like she does, but just because we have that bond doesn't mean I should fuck it up by doing something stupid.

A warm hand lands on my arm, pulling me from my thoughts. The hairs on my arm stand straight like another important part of me.

I don't have to look to know who it is, and that kind of scares me.

Because I know I'm going to do something to fuck this up. I just know it.

Ten

Makiya

I watch Hunter as he walks away from the field and climbs into his truck. I feel terrible, but what can I do?

I want to give him a chance, I desperately do, but I can't. I'm still hurting from everything that happened in our past and seeing him again only makes it worse.

Being abandoned by someone you love and thought you knew isn't something you can easily move on from. I still feel the pain as fresh as ever. I had wanted to believe I was over it, but it was never that simple.

I guess I need to work on that some more.

Little arms wrap around my leg, and I look down at Hannah.

My precious little girl. She deserves to know her father. Even if he broke my heart, it doesn't mean he would do the same to her. I know Hunter. He'd tried to build this strong, emotionless persona around him in high school, but I knew better then, just like I know better now.

And as much as he had tried to convince me this small-town life wasn't for him, I know it is. All he talked about when we were kids was what his family would be like someday. Then, suddenly, one day, he said he didn't want it anymore.

"Mommy, did you see me? I did so good today," Hannah says excitedly, bouncing up and down while still holding onto my leg.

"You were amazing out there tonight baby girl." I hug her the best I can since she only reaches my waist. I pack up the camping chair, grab her soccer bag and her hand, and walk to my old grey Honda Accord.

My Accord has been with me since high school. It had seen and done a lot of things with me over the years, but I'm afraid it's starting to see its last days. If the rust across the body isn't enough indication, then the sputtering of the exhaust and the random noises as I drive definitely is.

I load our stuff into the trunk and get Hannah buckled into her booster. She's old enough now that she can do it on her own, but thanks to my anxiety, I always check to make sure it's locked in place correctly.

I climb into the driver's side and start the short drive back to my dad's house. Country music plays softly in the background as I navigate the streets of our small town.

It doesn't take Hannah long before she asks the question I'd been dreading. "Mommy, why was that guy there tonight?"

And there it is. The one question I continue to have no idea how to answer.

How do I tell my baby girl that stranger came to watch her because he's her dad? I hate lying, especially to my daughter, but it's not the right time.

There may never be a right time. The words bounce around in my head. Words I'd heard my mother say countless times when I was growing up. But I push them aside, even if they may be true.

Sucking in a deep breath, I finally respond. "He's an old friend of mine. He was helping me at the cafe today, and I told him you had practice. He wanted to come watch." That's a good enough explanation. Vague, but truthful enough - at least I hope so.

"Okay." She pauses, fiddling with the seat belt that holds her into the booster seat.

"He seems nice. I think I like him," she states a few minutes later as she looks out the car window wistfully.

Well, that's a good thing. When I finally introduce him as her father, at least I'll know she likes him. Even if she ends up mad at me for not telling her.

Maybe it's a good thing he's back now rather than even farther down the road. I can't even begin to imagine what it would be like to tell a teenage Hannah.

I groan. Ugh, why did life have to be so damn complicated all the time?

Hannah stays quiet for the rest of our ride home. Once we're inside the house, I make her some dinner and then get her ready for bed, tuck her in, and read her a good night story.

This part of the day is always my favorite. It's the part where it's just me and Hannah. We read. We laugh. And I kiss her good night.

This time, though, it's different because I picture Hunter with me, sitting on the other side of Hannah. I read the story while he acts it out, and we laugh together. A family, just like I'd always wanted.

But it's just an image. An image that could be real if I would only let Hunter in again.

I make my way back downstairs to the kitchen after our bedtime rituals. I'm exhausted, but I live for these quiet moments after Hannah goes to sleep.

I pull a mug out of the cabinet next to the fridge and fish in the pantry for my special fruity tea mix. I make myself a cup of hot tea and sit down at the table.

What am I going to do?

I have to decide something soon, for Hannah *and* Hunter's sake. They both deserve a chance to know one another, and I know that.

I also know she has so many more questions about this strange man that looks just like her. She's too smart not to notice that he has the same features as her. Thankfully, she hasn't asked me about it yet, but it still doesn't make this situation any easier.

I take a small sip of tea to see if it has cooled down enough to let me drink it. I smile; it's not too hot or too cold, but just right. I take a larger sip and feel the soothing heat of the tea as it slides down the back of my throat.

After today, I need this more than anything to help me relax.

I hear the shuffling of feet coming down the hallway, and I desperately hope it isn't Hannah. She does that sometimes, especially when she's being stubborn. She'll ask for milk, water, say she's hungry, or that her belly hurts. Anything to not go to sleep right away.

Thankfully, it's not Hannah.

My dad enters the kitchen, and I startle him as I sit my cup down on the table. "I see you didn't realize I was in here."

"I thought you were still upstairs with Hannah. Clearly, I was wrong," he grunts as he reaches in the fridge for what I'm sure is at least his third beer of the night. My father loves his beer, especially after a long day of work at Hunter's family's construction company.

My dad has worked for Hunter's dad as long as I can remember. It's part of the reason we were so close growing up. Our dads had become good friends over the years, so it was only natural that we had, too.

"Sorry to disappoint, Dad, but I needed a cup of hot tea before I settled into bed."

"Rough day?" he asks, taking the seat to my left at the head of the table. My dad's always been intuitive. As a kid, he could tell how I was feeling just by looking at me. As frustrating as that is, it's nice to know he can still tell.

"You could say that. Had a surprise when I got to the café this morning." I pick up my cup of tea, letting it warm my hands and release the tension from my body as I breathe in its calming fragrance.

"Let me guess, your old pal Hunter showed up."

"My old pal? Really?" I laugh as my dad's face turns sour.

"What else am I supposed to call that no good son-of-a-bitch?"

I gasp. "Well, preferably something nicer than that."

My dad snorts as he lifts the beer to his mouth. "I thought that was pretty nice, considering."

My dad is rough around the edges, but he's a good man. I know he hates that Hunter broke my heart, even if he never actually said it to me. He's a man of few words, but I love him for that. He never needed to say much, especially not with me. I've always been able to tell what my dad's thinking simply from the expressions on his face, just like he can with me.

"I'll give you some credit. For you, that was fairly nice, considering I have fonder memories of you referring to him as much worse."

"Anyone who hurts my baby girl should be called much worse. I would have called him it to his face too, but I didn't figure you'd be very happy with me if I did."

I sit my teacup back down on the table and look at my dad's weathered and tanned face. He puts on a tough front for the world, but I've never doubted that he loves me, not once. For that, I'm beyond grateful.

"Yea, I probably wouldn't have, but I understand why you feel the way you do. It's the same reason I'm not sure letting him meet Hannah formally is a good idea."

"I ain't got no right to judge, nor am I any better a man than him, but I want ya to be careful and to consider all sides of this. He deserves to know his daughter, but he also has a bad track record. I get it."

I sigh as I stare at the older, male version of myself. "I know, and that's what makes this whole thing so difficult. I don't know what the right decision is, but I do know I need to protect Hannah. She's my life, and I won't let anyone hurt her."

My dad leans back in his chair and takes a long sip of his beer. "As much as I wanna hate him for what he did to y'all, I don't think he's capable of hurting her."

"But you can't know that!" I protest with a whine of frustration to my voice.

"No, I can't, just like you can't know that he *will* hurt her. There's no way to know what'll happen, princess, but there is one right way to deal with this, and you know exactly what that is." My dad places his hand on my arm, and my body relaxes at his familiar nickname for me.

I know he's right, but I also know the minute I decide to let him meet Hannah officially will be the same minute that my heart gets too attached again. I can't let that happen.

How can I protect myself and give Hannah and Hunter what they deserve at the same time?

I can't. It's as a simple as that. I know what I need to do because it's the *right* thing to do, but I don't like it.

Not one bit.

Eleven

Hunter

An hour later, I walk into my childhood home, following the hallway lined with pictures to the kitchen where my mom is leaning over a pan of...

Wait a hot minute!

I know that smell.

I would know that smell anywhere.

She's made her famous cornbread, which means it must be a special occasion.

After being gone for five years, I've forgotten how good my mom's cooking is, especially the cornbread. "Ma, is that your famous cornbread? It smells so good."

She turns to me and smiles. "Sure is. Made some beans to go with it."

I don't care what anyone says. My mom is by far the best out there.

"That sounds delicious." I lick my lips and walk closer to the stove, leaning over to take a whiff.

She smacks me with the spoon, and I retreat, just as I'd done a thousand times as a kid. Why is it that a wooden spoon is so much more frightening than my mother's bare hand?

The sting. It's definitely the sting it leaves.

I reach into the fridge and grab a beer. Popping the top off, I sit down in a chair at the table.

"Your brother should be here in a little bit with Meg," Mom tells me as she continues fixing dinner.

I take a swig of my beer. "Didn't realize they were comin' over."

"We haven't had a family dinner since you got back, so I invited them over. Your dad should be back soon, too," she says, stirring the beans one last time before turning the burner to low. She grabs a knife and slices the cornbread.

As she places the sliced cornbread on a plate, she asks in her thick Southern accent, "How was Hannah's practice tonight?"

I choke on the sip of beer I had just taken, spraying some of it across the table as I cough. "How did you know I was at Hannah's practice?"

"I hope you don't think I'm stupid, Hunter. I knew the minute you walked in and heard me talking to Ki that's where you were goin'. I hope to God she wasn't too upset."

I shake my head. "Surprisingly, she wasn't, or she was hiding it really well." I swallow another swig of beer, stealing myself against whatever comes out of my mother's mouth next.

My mom has no filter. In some ways, I was like that, too, and it had gotten me in trouble way too often as a kid. My damn mouth had even taken me to the principal's office more than a few times. But it's something I've been working on the last few years.

"I'm not surprised. She might deny it, but that girl still loves you." She shrugs her shoulders and places the plate of cornbread on the table in front of me.

I nearly choke again, and I haven't even taken another sip of my beer yet.

Yea, I definitely wasn't expecting her to say that.

"Love? Mom, what are you talkin' about? We were never in love," I scoff.

Right?

I mean we were kids. We'd been best friends our whole lives, but love?

Could we have been there at eighteen?

We hadn't even gone on any official dates, but I mean we were also almost always together.

My mom points the spoon she's holding in her hand at me. "I know what you're thinking, and maybe *you* weren't there, but she definitely was."

"Mom, we didn't even date."

She raises her eyebrows at me. "And your point is? Hunter, you'd been friends since you both started school. You knew each other better than anyone else. It doesn't matter that you hadn't 'officially' dated; she'd been in love with you since y'all were kids, and even now after you broke her heart into a million pieces, she still loves you."

I sit there silently, staring at her. What was I supposed to do with that?

I know there's still an attraction between us. That's lust though, not love.

I'd never really taken the time to think about it until now. I hadn't let myself get there, and maybe that's why I was here in this situation now.

Admitting is the first step, right?

The front door slams shut, and my brother and his fiancée greet us. "Hey, Mom," he says, giving her a kiss on the cheek.

He looks at me and bobs his head. "Hunter, it's good to see you."

I stand, walk to my older brother, and give him a hug. "It's good to see you too, Riley."

I turn to Meg and give her a kiss on the cheek. "It's been a long time, Meg, and you look as beautiful as ever."

Riley smacks me on the back of the head. "Dude, quit hitting on my woman."

I put my hands up in the air and laugh. "I wasn't hitting on your woman, but glad to see she has you whipped."

He waves his hand in front of him. "I'm not whipped. I'm just a very jealous man. Right, honey?" he asks his girl as he puts his arm around her.

She laughs, then looks at me. "It's true. He gets upset when my brothers give me hugs." She rolls her eyes. Riley and Meg claim their seats at the table, and I sit back down in mine.

It had been way too long since I've seen my brother. He's a couple years older than me, but we'd always been pretty close. He works with my dad at the construction company, and he'd tried to convince me to join them before I came back, but I hadn't planned on sticking around that long. Now, that plan has changed.

Riley glances over at Mom pulling glasses out of the cabinet. "Where's dad?"

Mom places the glasses in a line on the counter and sets out some drinks from the fridge. "He should be back any minute."

As Mom finishes the final touches for dinner and Riley and I catch up, we hear the rumble of dad's work truck pulling into the driveway.

Dad walks through the back door that leads right into the kitchen, dirt and grime covering his old flannel work shirt. He gives Mom a kiss on his way to the sink, where he washes his hands, like he does every night, before taking a seat at the table.

"Where's Ki and Hannah?" Dad asks as he opens his beer.

Mom's wide eyes move between me and Dad. "Um, she said she couldn't make it tonight." I feel Dad's eyes on me as Mom speaks.

I love my old man, but we have never seen things eye to eye. I know now will be no different.

I brace myself for the comments to come, but all he says is, "That's a shame." And I agree with him.

Because he's right.

It is a damn shame.

Twelve

Hunter

I step through the back door of the café at half past five in the morning. I'm still half asleep, and my body feels like it was hit by a truck. I barely had the energy to get dressed let alone come to the café, but I promised Ki I'd be here.

So, here I am, standing in the back door looking like a zombie. Honestly, I'm not even sure what I look like; I threw on some clothes and brushed my teeth, not even stopping to look in the mirror.

"You're late!" Ki yells from inside the kitchen. I haven't even made it to the kitchen door yet thanks to my sorry excuse of a body.

When did I become so out of shape that one day of work made me feel like death? I never imagined that helping in the café would be so tiring.

I make my way slowly into the kitchen and apologize to Ki for being late. She's lucky I'm here at all.

"You look like shit," she says, handing me a cup of coffee. I've never been so thankful to see coffee in my life.

"Gee, thanks," I drain the cup, ignoring the burn of the hot liquid as it scorches my throat and hand it back to her.

She looks from the cup to me then back. "You're not tired, are you?" Sarcasm drips with every word and a sexy smirk makes its way on to her lips.

"Of course not," I scoff. She thinks she's funny, but she's not.

She laughs as she refills the cup and hands it back to me. "You're a terrible liar. Have another cup, I promise you'll start feeling more like a human being after you finish it." She goes back to working on the pastries in front of her.

I sit down on the bar stool on the other side of the large stainless-steel table in the middle of the kitchen. "Thanks for this," I say, sipping a little slower this time around.

She rolls, shapes, and places the pastries on the baking sheet to the left of her. She handles the dough so carefully almost like it's a delicate piece of glass. "This job is a lot harder than it looks. The early mornings are the worst part."

"No kidding, I thought I was dying when my alarm went off this morning. I fell back to sleep without even realizing it."

"Yea, I felt that way the first few weeks I started working here with Mom. You get used to it eventually, just takes time for your body to adjust." She continues rolling and shaping the dough delicately, a soft, peaceful smile on her face as she fills the sheet with pastries.

I watch with fascination at how she takes such gentle care with each one. "Did your mom teach you how to make these?"

"Yea, I used to spend every Saturday baking with her growing up. Then, after I found out I was pregnant, I came to work here full time." She pauses, glancing up at me and searching my eyes. "Sorry, was that insensitive?"

"No, Ki," I assure her. "You can tell me stories about that time. Actually, I'd love to hear them. Makes me feel like I didn't miss as much as I did."

"Okay," she smiles shyly before going back to work on the pastries.

"I guess you didn't make it to college then?"

She shakes her head as she places the last pastry on the sheet. She brushes the flour off her hands and carries the tray to the oven. Placing it carefully inside, she sets the timer before coming back to the table. "No, I didn't. Sometimes, I wish I had, but other times I'm grateful that I didn't. I wouldn't have been able to do all this if I had." She waves the towel in her hands around the kitchen.

"If you could go back, what would you have studied?"

She stops to think for a minute. "I don't think I would go back. I mean if I had the opportunity I might go for business, but Mom taught me everything I needed to know to run this place before she got sick. Plus, Dad helps out with the business side of things when he can."

"You know I could help with the business side if you need it?"

She raises her eyebrows at me. "Oh really?"

She probably thinks I'm only suggesting it to get out of doing the hard work. And she's right, I am, but I'm also pretty good at business.

I shrug my shoulders, pretending it isn't a big deal to me either way. "I may have gotten my degree in business and paid attention in a few classes."

"If you could, that would be great. I do okay with the business stuff but baking and cooking are more my passion."

At least she doesn't make a comment about me being a big baby for offering to work in the office, even though it would be deserved.

She looks to the clock as the back door opens. Sabrina comes bounding in and stops short when her eyes land on me. "Oh, Hunter. What are you doing here?"

Ki steps in to speak before I can respond. "He's going to be helping us with the business stuff since I suck at it." She turns to me.

"If you want to work on that today, everything is on the desk in the office. If you have any questions, I can try to help."

I take the hint and stand to head back towards the office. "I should be able to find everything, but if I need you, I'll holler."

I stop just inside the office door, listening to what's being said in the kitchen.

"Are you nuts, Ki? Why is he here?" Sabrina screeches in a loud whisper.

"You're guess is as good as mine. He showed up yesterday and helped out after you called in sick. He said he'd be back today, and honestly, I could use his help. By the way, are you feeling better?"

"Yea, just some food poisoning I think, but that's beside the point. Ki, I just want you to be careful. I don't want to see you hurt again because of him," Sabrina says less hysterically this time.

"I know, but he's Hannah's father, and he says he's sticking around. If that's the truth, I have no choice. I can't keep him from me and Hannah forever."

"I just hope you know what you're doing."

"Yea, me too." Ki ends the conversation with some banging in the kitchen.

Five Years Ago

I had every intention of taking Ki to the field party like we've done every Friday night for two years, but the minute I saw her, I knew I couldn't handle all the guys from the team staring at her all night. And not just because she looked so damn hot in her painted-on jeans and fiery red flannel shirt, but because she was doing things to me - things I wasn't sure I could ignore any longer.

I knew if I took her to that party and I saw one person checking her out, there were going to be words.

That's why I drive straight past the field party and on to our spot in the middle of the swamp.

"Um, where are we going?" she asks, pointing her thumb behind her. "The party is back there."

"Yea, I know, but I'm not feeling the party tonight." I say, shrugging my shoulders and reminding myself to breathe when I glance over my shoulder at her.

She knows something is up. I can tell from the crinkle in her brow and the way she purses her lip like she just ate something sour.

"Okay," she says slowly not sounding convinced. "Then, where are we going?"

"I thought we could go to our spot."

"Why? There's nothing to see at night. It's too dark. Plus, we only go there to watch the sunrise."

"Exactly. We can watch the stars."

I know her mind isn't even on the same track as mine. She's so innocent, always has been, but I can't help the direction my mind has taken ever since it realized Ki wasn't just a girl anymore.

I want so badly to touch her, hold her in a way that's far more than a "just friends" action, but I don't know if it's a good idea. I'm going off to school next week to start football camp, and she's staying here until the fall.

And I know she's not the one-night-stand type of girl. Plus, she's my best friend. Making any kind of move would be just plain stupid, but I don't know if I can hold myself back. Not just because she's fucking gorgeous on the outside, but because she's not once ever left my side.

I don't care if that makes me sound like a pussy. I'm just being sentimental, thinking about all the ways this girl has changed my life and made it better and knowing I might lose it all when we go our separate ways.

I pull off the dirt road into a little patch of grass. Ki hops out of the truck like she's done so many times before, and I follow.

When I make it around to the bed of the truck, I notice she's still standing by the passenger door, her head points to the sky and a smile spreads across her face.

She looks over her shoulder, her smile growing wider. "You know what? This was a much better idea. I've never seen the stars so bright."

And I've never seen her face shine so bright.

I know Sabrina is just being protective of her long-time best friend, but I can't deny that her words rock me to the core, like a punch to the gut.

When I left five years ago, I didn't think I was doing that much damage. Actually, I thought I was doing Ki a favor by leaving earlier than planned, keeping her from getting her heart broken, but now I know I was just protecting my own.

It's a lot easier to place the blame on Ki, though, than it is to admit that I'm a chicken.

The more I think about the past, the more I realize that maybe I had been sabotaging the whole thing because I was getting too close to Ki. My feelings for her had grown stronger than I knew what to do with, so I ran with the excuse of a football scholarship.

Yet, after all of that, I had still ended up hurting myself in the long run. I missed out on seeing my daughter grow.

Yea, I'd definitely messed that one up for myself, but dwelling on the past wouldn't change it. Instead, I needed to focus on the future, which currently involves learning about the business of running a café.

I walk over to the mess of an office desk and begin sorting through the papers and invoices on top of it. Ki wasn't kidding when she said she wasn't too great with the business side.

I set into putting things in order as the day ticks by. I make stacks on the desk in categories, check the numbers in the books, and

I even look back at the café's financial history. A knock on the door pulls me out of the paperwork I'm sorting.

"I thought you might be hungry," Ki says, laying a sandwich down on the desk in front of me.

"Thanks, what time is it?" I ask, studying the delicious-looking turkey and cheese sandwich sitting in front of me.

"A little after one." *Huh, I hadn't realized it was that late already.*

"Time to close up shop soon."

"Yea, I have to pick up Hannah from school at three." She shifts from one foot to the other and avoids looking me in the face.

I can't help but wonder what's going on in that pretty little head of hers. I hope she's thinking about letting me go with her to pick Hannah up, but that's a long shot I know I'm going to miss.

Still, she looks extremely nervous. Maybe it *is* what she's thinking about after all.

"You okay?" I question, slightly concerned about the way her face is twisted up.

She nods her head still avoiding my gaze. "I thought maybe you'd like to come pick Hannah up with me."

"Hell yea!" My heart feels like it could beat out of my chest.

Damn, I definitely didn't expect to hear those words today, but they are music to my ears.

"Okay, I'll let you get back to work. We can leave when everything is closed up."

"I'll be here." I smile and take a bite of the massive sandwich in front of me.

This is easily the highlight of my year. *I'm finally going to spend time with my daughter*, I think to myself.

But, will she tell her who I am?

Now, *that's* the real question.

Thirteen

Makiya

My pulse races the closer we get to Sunrise Elementary School. Hunter had insisted on driving, but I insisted on taking my beat up, old Honda, knowing that Hannah wouldn't recognize Hunter's truck.

I can't believe I'm following through with this invite. *Am I insane?*

"So, Ki, I know this is a step forward, but I'm curious."

Oh no. I know what question's coming next. It's the question I'd been dreading since I'd invited him to come with me. The one question I still don't know how to answer.

He can ask me anything else. Just, please, not that question.

"Are you going to tell her today?"

Ugh. I close my eyes and groan. Come on, God, you couldn't answer just one plea from me.

Life is never going to go back the way it was before Hunter knew, I have to accept that.

Opening my eyes again, I give Hunter the sternest face I can muster. "If you hurt her, I swear I will hunt you down and kill you. Do you understand me?"

He gives me the biggest smile – a truly genuine smile. "I hear you loud and clear, Ki, and I promise I won't hurt her."

I fight the urge to laugh; I know no number of promises will ease the reality of the situation. He'd left before, he could do it again, but I know I can't keep him from his daughter any longer. "I hope you know what you're promising."

Being a parent is hard work. Some days are great. Other days, you feel like nothing you do is right. You can't make promises you couldn't keep. I'm not so sure Hunter understands that concept, but hopefully I'm wrong.

He sighs as he pulls into the parking lot of the elementary school. We're a little early for pickup, but I'm always early on purpose. I try to make sure I get a parking space close to the door so I can watch Hannah as she comes out of school.

"This may surprise you, Ki, but I do know what I'm doing. I know this is a big deal, I get it, and I want to be there for you and for

Hannah any way I can." His hands clench the steering wheel in a death grip.

"It's not some fairy tale fantasy you get to live out, Hunter. This is real life. It's hard raising a child, especially one as stubborn as Hannah. You know that last night she spent forty-five minutes fighting with me about taking a bath? A bath which she desperately needed after soccer practice?"

He pinches the bridge of his nose and closes his eyes. "No, I didn't know that because I wasn't there, and that's the reason I want to be there. I want to fight with her about taking a bath or going to bed or whatever other things she fights with you about in a day. I want to be her father, Ki. I already missed out on so much, I won't miss out on anything more."

I hear his words. I feel them deep within my soul, and I know he means what he says by the tight grip of his hands on the steering wheel and his clenched jaw.

No matter how much I want to push him away and keep my heart safe, this isn't just about me.

He's missed out on so much of Hannah's life, and Hannah has missed out on knowing her dad. It doesn't matter whose fault it is anymore.

"I know. It's just so hard for me," I confess. Being vulnerable with Hunter scares me, but it feels right. I feel at home with him, I always have.

"I understand that, I know I made mistakes. I know I hurt you. I wish I could go back and do things differently, but we can't change the past. Doesn't mean I don't want to change the future."

I sigh. He makes sense. I can't change the past. I've spent so many nights agonizing over the fact that Hannah would never know her father. The future I had seen included just me and Hannah, but I have the power to change that now. I just need to stop being so selfish.

Because that's what I am. I'm selfish. I don't want to share Hannah with him. I don't want him to have another piece of me that he could break. She's my everything.

I suck in a breath and stare out the front windshield. "When I was pregnant, I waited for this moment. I hoped that you would come back to see me, and you'd find out. I wanted you to know your daughter. I wanted you to be there for all of it, but you never came back. The longer you were away, the more I realized that you weren't coming back. Then, one day, you show up, and everything I reconciled with went up in smoke."

I turn to face him. I need him to see the turmoil I'm facing inside, the sting of his actions and the pulse of an anxious heart. "I accepted the fact that Hannah wouldn't know you. I accepted the fact that we were over, but here you are sitting in the front seat of my car. Everything changed overnight, and I don't know how to deal with that. I'd taught myself to hate you, but now, I have to learn not to again. Which, I will admit, is easier than I thought it would be."

Hunter laughs at my last admission, but I can see the sadness and regret in his eyes. He feels my agony, and I'm glad because I need him to know why I'm being so cautious. "I'm sorry I left. I don't know how many more times I have to say that, but I was running. I was scared."

"Running from what?" I unbuckle my seatbelt so I can look at him better.

"I didn't know at the time, but now, I think I do. I was running from us, from the feelings I had for you because they terrified me. There was so much I wanted to do with my life - I didn't want to get married right out of high school and work for my father like my parents had done. I wanted to play professional football, to travel the country, and see all the things I hadn't seen as a kid."

"I knew that. Why do you think I let you go without a fight? Why do you think I didn't try harder to tell you about Hannah? I knew then that you didn't want this life, at least not then. Your mom knew, too. That's why when I came back to her car crying that day, she drove away and promised to keep my secret. You were always a free-spirit that needed your chance to fly," I speak softly, twisting my fingers together.

Hunter catches one of my hands in his. "I had my chance to fly, and it wasn't what I wanted, not even close. You've given me plenty of time to change my mind, Ki, but I haven't. I want this. I want to be her father."

A tear slides down my cheek and I choke on a sob. *Vulnerability sucks*. It hurts so bad, but it's also so freeing. It's like a weight I had been carrying for the last five years was finally lifted off my shoulders.

Just then, the doors to the school open and the students pour out. I look at Hunter. "Guess it's now or never," I say as I get out of the car and lean against the door.

Now or never.

I still want to vote never.

Fourteen

Hunter

When I came with Ki today, the one thing I hadn't expected was for her to agree to tell Hannah. I expected to have to fight harder before I won that battle, but I've never been more excited to be wrong.

Hannah bounds through the doors of the school and heads straight for us, and suddenly my excitement turns to nerves. What the hell am I supposed to do? What do I say?

I don't know anything about her.

I wipe my sweaty palms against the side of my dark denim jeans.

Shit, this is way more than I bargained for. Maybe Ki was right and I'm not ready for this. My nerves surge faster through my body. All I want to do is run, but my feet won't move. I'm frozen in place, panic spreading through my body.

Hannah moves closer to us, and my heart feels like it's about to beat out of my chest. What if I'm not good enough to be a dad? Hell, I don't even know how to *be* a dad. I mean I have a really good one, so maybe I should just channel him.

And just like that, I'm officially way too overwhelmed to handle this situation. Doubts swirl around inside my head. *What the fuck was I thinking?*

Hannah looks at me, the same eyes I see in the mirror every morning staring back at me now in front of a school. Her curly red hair hangs around her curious face. God, she looks so innocent, so tiny. I'm terrified that I'm going to ruin this entire moment.

Then, she smiles at me, and the racing of my heart slows to a steadier pace. *I can do this.*

"You're that man that keeps following Mommy around." The way she says it makes me sound like a damn stalker. I'm glad no one is around us to hear it.

I nod, kneeling down in front of her. "Yes, I am."

She turns to Ki and tugs on her mom's hand. "Mom, me and him have the same color hair."

Ki smiles softly at her. "Yea, baby girl, you do." She sucks in a breath, and I can only imagine how she must be feeling right now. "Hannah, sweetheart, Mommy needs to tell you something."

"Okay," Hannah says with her face scrunched together in a serious look.

I watch the scene unfold as Ki squats down in front of Hannah. I don't know where I'm supposed to be in this conversation, so I stand and take a step back. Ki and I aren't a unit which I regret a lot. I should have been there for her.

Instead, all I can do is watch Hannah's face as Ki prepares to tell her about me. The dad she never knew. The dad who walked out on her mom for some dumbass football career. Not that Hannah is old enough to understand any of that.

Hell, maybe she does understand. I don't know.

I hate myself for doing this. I created this shit fest by leaving and jumping into bed with the first girl who fell all over me at college. I was a confused, hormone-controlled kid who believed sex and parties were what made you happy.

But none of it ever had.

Ki kneels so she's face to face with Hannah. "I know you're curious about who he is 'cause you've seen him around a lot lately," she says.

Hannah scrunches her lips together. "Yea."

Ki laughs softly, glancing back at me and taking a deep breath. "Hannah, this is Hunter. He's your dad."

A swirl of confusion floats across Hannah's face. "*That's* my dad?" she asks, sounding more disgusted than confused.

Man, does she have a way with words. I can't help the sudden pain in my heart at the way Hannah says *dad* or the sour look she has on her face.

Ki's voice goes soft. "Yea, honey, he's your dad."

Hannah chews on her bottom lip as she seems to think about that fact.

Hannah turns to me. Her eyebrows scrunch together in confusion and she looks at me curiously. She tilts her head to the side studying my face. I can tell she wants to say something.

Ki pushes her forward with her hand, a silent bit of encouragement. Then, she whispers something in Hannah's ear that makes her laugh.

Hannah walks slowly towards me. Her face wrinkles with a fierceness so much like Ki's it makes my heart race.

Shit, my little girl kind of scares me. I rest a hand over my heart, willing it to slow down just a little bit.

"Does this mean I have to call you Dad?" Hannah asks.

I laugh without thinking. Then, I see her eyes, slowly fill with tears and my heart hurts even more. Shit, what did I do? I never meant to hurt her.

Quickly, I bend down to her level. "Hannah, you can call me whatever you want to."

She nods her little head at me and folds her arms in front of her. For five years old, she has one hell of an attitude. "Good." At least my answer seems to satisfy her.

Glancing back to her mom, she asks her something about dinner which I miss because I'm too focused on watching Hannah.

Ki nods. "If he wants too, sure."

Hannah turns back to me. "Do you want to have dinner with us?"

I'm so happy I don't even know what to say, but I'm sure the smile across my face says it all for me.

I glance to Ki for her approval. She gives me a slight nod even though there's a frown on her face.

I know she's scared, but I'm not going anywhere. Not this time.

"Sure," I respond to my daughter.

My daughter.

I still can't believe it.

Her face lights up, and I know with every part of me that this is where I want to be right now.

Fifteen

Makiya

The last thing I'd expected to do today was to have Hunter over to the house for dinner.

Actually, I take that back. The last thing I'd expected to do today was to introduce Hannah to Hunter.

Yet somehow, I'd done both.

Thankfully, though, my dad is having dinner with his friends tonight, which means no dad drama at dinner. That takes a little of the pressure off, but I'm still stressed.

How will this dinner turn out?

What will Hannah want to know about her father?

Will she like him? Will he like her?

Will things like this continue to happen?

Oh, I hope so - for mine and Hannah's sake. Because after this dinner, Hannah will be all in.

I place the large bowl of salad on the table along with the rolls. I go back to the oven and pull out the lasagna Hannah had requested for dinner and carry it over to the table, putting it in the center. The table isn't large and barely holds all the food and three place settings, but I manage to fit it all on there.

I walk back to the counter to grab the serving utensils I'd pulled out earlier. I reach for them and turn to head back to the table, but Hunter's laugh stops me.

Well, not just Hunter's laugh, but Hannah's, too. I watch the interaction between the two of them, both laughing.

A full-on, rolling on the floor kind of laugh.

"What's so funny over there?" I ask as I make my way over to the table. I lay the utensils down and take the seat across from Hannah and Hunter.

She had insisted on sitting next to him when they sat down at the table. Which I *think* is a good thing.

"It's a secret." Hannah puts her forefinger up to her lips.

"Well, I see how it is." I pucker my lips into a pout.

"Sorry, mama," she says, her tone nonchalant like she isn't actually sorry.

Well, fine then. I don't care.

Except, I really do care. A lump forms at the back of my throat. They're sharing secrets already.

I can't be jealous. Hannah needs this. It's a good thing.

"Honestly, Ki, it's nothing," Hunter assures me with a tip of his head. I appreciate that he picks up on how I'm feeling.

"Okay, okay," I mutter, reaching to cut the lasagna. "If ya'll want food, you better start dishing it out."

Once everyone's plates are full, Hannah situates herself in her chair so she's facing Hunter. She chews intently on a piece of bread before swallowing swiftly and asking, "Can we play a game?"

Hunter glances my way and I shrug my shoulders. I don't have any clue where this is leading either.

"Well, what kind of game is it? Maybe we can play it after dinner," he answers.

She shakes her head, unsatisfied with his answer. "No, it's a question game. We can play it now."

"Question game?"

She nods and chews on another bite of her roll while squishing the rest of it in her hand. "I ask you questions and then you ask me some."

"So, like twenty questions?"

I giggle. Hannah has no idea what that game is, and Hunter can tell by her quirked eyebrows and scrunched nose. She thinks on it a few more seconds and her mouth curls down into a frown. "I don't know if it will be twenty questions."

Hunter lets out a small chuckle. "Ask away, Hannah."

She sits up straight, puts her roll on her plate, and brushes the crumbs off her hands. "What's your name?"

"Hunter."

She sighs. "No, your whole name?"

"Oh, right, Hunter James Hart."

Hannah looks over to me. "Does that mean I have to change my name mama?"

"No, baby, it doesn't, but you do have to eat your dinner." I point to the still nearly full plate sitting in front of her.

She rolls her eyes back at me. I would never hit Hannah, but I really want to smack the attitude out of her sometimes. I swear I don't know how my mama raised me if I acted like this, and I know I did.

She looks back to Hunter and begins her inquisition again, ever the little warrior princess. "What's your favorite color?"

"Brown," he answers, gazing into my eyes.

Nice. One point for Hunter in the suck up category.

Hannah scrunches her face up in disgust. "Eww, why?"

"Because they're the color of your mama's eyes. Why? What is your favorite color?" Oh, if Hunter keeps it up, I may have to kick him out of this house. Just so I don't do something stupid. Flattery won't get him anywhere.

Yet.

"Green," Hannah says with a quick nod of her head. "What's your favorite movie?"

"Um, I don't know. I like a lot of movies. Some I'm sure you aren't allowed to watch." He pops his finger on her nose.

She smacks it away. "Don't distract me," she squeals.

Yea, I taught her that one, and I'm not ashamed to admit it.

She looks back at Hunter pointedly. "Do you like princesses?"

Hannah stares up at him, waiting for his response. "Sure, I like princesses," he manages to squeeze out without choking on a laugh.

"Liar," I whisper, putting my hand up conspiratorially.

"Please, don't tell her that," he whispers back.

I laugh as Hannah continues her game, unphased by our brief interruption.

"Good," Hannah nods. "Now, Mama said you had to leave when I was a baby because it was important. Where did you have to go?"

Hunter freezes, his fork an inch from his face with lasagna threatening to slide off any second.

My heart pounds. I wasn't expecting her to ask a question like that either.

I stand and walk across to the other side of the table. I place my hands on Hunter's shoulders, trying to soothe him. Finally, he places his fork back down on the plate.

I move around him and squat down in front of Hannah. "Your dad went to college so he could come back and help us with the café like he's doing now."

"But why didn't he take us with him?" she frowns.

"Because Mama needed to stay here to take care of you."

I'm lying to her. I know that, and I hate it, but the need to protect my daughter from rejection is far stronger than my need to be honest.

I feel Hunter's hand on my shoulder. He whispers in my ear, "Thank you for that."

I point to Hannah's plate. "Why don't we stop with the questions for now, okay? Let's finish dinner. I'm sure you can ask him a bunch more questions when you see him again."

"Fine," Hannah whines, but she does as I ask.

Yea, this is definitely *not* what I expected today.

Sixteen

Hunter

A couple hours later, Ki walks me out to the back porch. She had let me say good night to Hannah before she took her upstairs, but she told me not to leave while she put Hannah to bed.

And I'm glad I didn't.

I needed that extra time to process everything that happened at dinner, especially the last question she'd asked.

I hadn't been expecting that. I don't know why. I mean it's the first question I'd want to ask the dad I'd never met, but she just seems so innocent, so carefree like it's something that hadn't really bothered her.

Obviously, it had, not that I blame her, but our light and fun conversation hadn't prepared me for the heavy question.

It came out of nowhere, wanting to know why I left her, where I went.

I didn't have any idea what to say, but then, Ki had come to my rescue, and I had been so grateful.

After everything that's happened today, I honestly don't know if I can handle this "dad" stuff. Am I really cut out for it?

I mean, I didn't even know how to answer my daughter's question, and I know there will be more just like it. I was gone for too long. How can she not have more questions like that?

I've never felt more regret than I do right now. Nothing I've accomplished in life could ever make that look of pain and rejection in Hannah's eyes go away.

Ki motions for me to have a seat in one of the chairs on the porch while she sits in the other. We look out over the backyard, a perfect sunset in front of us. I'm amazed at the different shades that fill the sky, and it takes me back to another night almost like this.

That Night

It's perfect. This whole fucking night is perfect. *I remind myself before I do something completely stupid like kiss my best friend.*

"Hunter?" she asks softly against the coastal breeze.

Our spot isn't far from the beach. It's nestled in the marshes just off the coast, and I don't even know how we found this place. You have to take a random dirt road to get back in here.

All I know is when we did find this spot, Ki fell in love and insisted we needed to come here at least once a week to watch the sunrise. Of course, that convincing came long after our night on the roof at her house.

She's the only person I'd ever wake up at 4 AM for to watch the damn sun rise.

"Hunter?" she whispers again, capturing my full attention.

I glance down at her cuddled up in my arms. It's the look in her eyes that gets me first – a mixture of love, lust, and pure trust.

I can't stop myself from reacting. I capture her lips in mine. At first, she hesitates, but it only takes a second for her to fall into my kiss.

I force her lips open with my tongue, deepening our connection. She moans softly, grabbing onto my shirt and pulling herself closer.

She has no idea what she does to me. No fucking clue.

I pull her onto my lap, needing her closer to me. My fingers weave themselves into her long hair, bringing her closer more and more each passing moment.

She whispers my name against my lips and need surges through me. "Don't stop," she mutters.

Her words catch me off guard, but they're all I need to hear.

I slip my hands from her hair and down to her waist, flipping her onto her back. I slowly unbutton her flannel shirt, pulling it down her arms and tossing it to the side.

I slide my hands up and down her waist, reveling in the feel of her. I move my lips from hers and trail soft kisses down her neck and chest.

"Are you sure about this?" I ask before I reach to pull off her tank top.

"I've never been more sure," she says softly.

I must be dreaming. I have to be because there's no way any of this could possibly be real. I mean this only ever happens in my dreams.

Ki situates herself so she can face me. "You know I imagined this day a hundred times, but I never thought it would be like that," she says quietly, sweeping her hand through her long brown hair.

I'm kind of shocked that she'd even imagined this day at all, not after her and my mother's confessions that I was never even supposed to know.

"What did you imagine?" I can't help myself; I have to know.

She shrugs her shoulders and sits silently for a minute, lost in her thoughts.

I study her long face and her short nose, noticing the dimples on the sides of her lips from her clenched jaw. She always does that when she's anxious - a bad habit that causes her a lot of headaches, or at least, it used to.

I'm curious once again about the thoughts floating through her mind. She looks so angry and tense. I want to go to her, to comfort her, but I don't think I've earned that right back just yet.

It hurts like hell though, watching the different emotions play out on her face and knowing that I'm part of the reason they're there.

She continues to stare out at the sunset and finally speaks. "I guess I always thought that it would be Hannah that would force me to contact you when she was older. She's always been curious, like a blazing fire was lit inside her. That fire has always scared me. I knew that one day she would insist on meeting you, and I would have no choice but to find you. If I didn't, *she* would."

"So, what you're saying is, she's too much like you?"

She sighs. "She looks just like you and that always bothered me, but as she gets older, her personality shows more and more." Ki laughs softly. "She might have your looks, but she is all me."

"Yea, she definitely is." Even with the little time I've spent with Hannah, it's easy to see the resemblance between their personalities.

From what I've seen of Hannah though, I wouldn't want her any other way. Her fiery passion was so evident at dinner. Her determination to learn everything about me in such a short time was admirable.

If I'd had even a little bit of her passion as a kid, I might not be where I am today.

Silence fills the space between us again, but only for a minute before Ki breaks it. "Are you mad at me?"

"No," I answer quickly, honestly.

I want to be mad at her more than anything. And at first, I *was* mad at her and my mom, but I've realized it's not only their fault. It's mine, too. Ki had tried to tell me, even if it was a futile attempt. She could have tried harder, and maybe she should have, but I have to give her credit for at least trying.

I'm angrier at myself more than anyone else.

I had screwed up.

I made a bad decision that, at the time, I thought would make me happy.

I was wrong though.

Completely and totally wrong.

Losing my dream of playing professional football taught me to be grateful for what I had. So, as much as I want to hate her for lying, I'll never be able to.

Because if I'm being honest, I've lied too.

About the real reason I left. The real reason I hadn't come back until now.

Seventeen

Makiya

How can he not be angry with me? I find it very hard to believe. I'd kept his daughter away from him for the first part of her life. He has every right to be angry with me.

I'd be angry with myself if I were him. Hell, I *am* angry with myself. I never meant to hurt him. I just wanted to protect myself and Hannah.

."Don't get me wrong," he says, almost reading my thoughts. "I'm not happy that you kept her from me, and I'm not happy with my mom either, but the person I'm mad at most is myself." He speaks those last few words so softly I barely hear them.

He's angry with himself? How does that make sense? None of this is his fault. Okay, maybe a lot of it is his fault, but keeping Hannah a secret, that was all on me.

"You shouldn't be mad at yourself, Hunter," I say truthfully. I had spent years holding one simple thing against him.

Sure, it hurt me like hell, and yea, it feels kind of good knowing he feels the pain now, but I shouldn't have kept such a big secret from him.

Right?

"Why not? If I hadn't been so set on leaving this town, I would have been here for you, or at the least, I would have come back to visit." His head hangs low, touching his chin to his chest. He looks so ashamed.

"You needed to leave. If you'd stayed, you would have regretted it. You would have always wondered what could have happened." I suck in a breath.

It's true.

It's taken me five years to see it, but he wasn't happy here. Not then.

Now, though, it seems like he is. Like maybe this had been his real dream all along.

"You needed to see if you could make your dream come true. You wouldn't have been happy here." And I actually believe what I'm saying, too.

"You don't know that Ki," he bites out.

But I do know that. Regret is a powerful thing.

One that would have led him away from me eventually.

A part of me, the part still in love with him, wants to reach for him. To comfort him. To hold him.

I hold back though, clenching my fists together.

I try to remember the anger I had felt only hours before, the blood boiling in my veins, but I can't deny the difference between the man from my past and the man in front of me now.

He's not the same Hunter, and I can't keep holding that against him.

I look back out at the sunset.

"Do you ever wonder what would have happened if we'd actually started dating?" I ask, softly.

He sighs deeply. "Of course, I do. I wonder every day what would have happened if I hadn't been so damn stubborn. You were my best friend, and I was too terrified to fuck that up."

"Yea," I whisper into the soft breeze.

He reaches for my hand. "You know that night was the best night of my life."

I see the truth as bright as can be in his green eyes.

"For me, too. I was so surprised when you, of all people, suggested going out to our spot to watch the stars. It was just so unlike you."

"Yea, I wasn't really myself that night. Seeing you all dressed up and finally acknowledging the feelings I'd been forcing back made me all kinds of crazy." He chuckles.

I laugh along with him, but it stings a bit knowing that if he'd made a move sooner, maybe we could have made it. Maybe none of this would have happened.

I know that things could have been different, but I also knew Hunter, and how he needed the chance to find himself. I'm not sure if that's what he's done or not, but the man sitting next to me isn't the same boy I knew when we were kids.

He's different.

Wiser, maybe.

I can't quite put my finger on it.

What I do know is that if this had been the Hunter here five years ago, we would be in a very different place right now.

Everything that happened today never would have needed to happen.

I wonder about that a lot.

The day I went to tell him.

The Day that Changed Everything

We pull into the parking space outside his dorm. I suck in a deep breath, pressing my hand against my stomach.

Never in my wildest dreams did I think this is where I'd be at the end of summer – telling the boy who left me after one night of pure bliss that I'm pregnant.

"Are you sure you don't want me to come with you?" Hunter's mom asks from the driver's seat.

It's weird coming here with his mom, but she's the only one who knew where he was living.

Plus, I couldn't come with my own mom. She'd have killed him before I even got to tell him about the baby. She's that pissed off. She says it's not because he got me pregnant, but that he left without a word a week earlier than he was supposed to – the day after our night together.

If I'm being honest with myself, that's the part that pisses me off the most, too.

I glance at the woman who's supported me so much more than she ever needed to. "Yea, I need to do this alone."

She reaches for my hand. "You've got this. Just tell him the truth, and whatever happens, happens. We'll figure it out."

Her words comfort me more than she could ever know. I nod at her and open the door. Stepping out onto the pavement, I breathe in deeply, taking in the smell of freshly mown grass. It's not my favorite smell, but the deep breath helps calm my racing heart a bit.

I turn towards the building and head inside. I have no clue which room is Hunter's, so I stop at the desk just inside the dorm where an RA sits.

"Hello, how can I help you today?" The slim woman asks with a friendly smile.

"Yes, I'm looking for Hunter Hart. He never told me what room he's in, just the building." I hope my lie is fairly convincing.

The RA nods with a knowing smile. "Ah, yes, he seems to be very popular on campus, especially with the cheerleaders. Unfortunately, I can't tell you what his room number is, but you're welcome to see if you can find him," she says.

A sharp pang hits my heart, and I fight the urge to run out of the building. Is there any point in telling him about the baby if his room is already a revolving door of cheerleaders?

The worst part is I know it's true. It's how he was in high school, too.

Not to mention, how the hell am I supposed to find his room? "Thank you," I respond even though she wasn't helpful at all.

I head down the first hallway, hoping there might be names on the doors or something, but I don't see any.

Well, that's just great! *I scream inside my head.*

I keep walking down the halls, thinking maybe I'll get lucky and run into him or someone who knows him. It's the only option I have since he hasn't answered my phone calls or texts over the last couple months.

A door slams from behind me, and I jump at the sound. "I do believe I've never seen you around here before," a deep voice chuckles.

I turn slowly on my heels, knowing the voice isn't Hunter's and also knowing I have no choice but to ask this guy if he knows him. "Yea, um, I'm actually looking for someone." *I stammer, my voice shaking with nervousness.*

"Well, you found him, then." *He smirks in such a devious way.*

I want to give him all kinds of sass, but I don't have it in me right now. My nerves about telling Hunter are too strong. "Do you know which room is Hunter Hart's?" *I ask instead.*

His smirk turns into a chuckle. "As a matter of fact, he's my neighbor." *He points his thumb at the room next to his.* "But I don't think you want to talk to him at the moment."

I'm so grateful to have found Hunter's room that I don't even think about the guy's comment.

I make my feet move past him so I'm standing in front of Hunter's door. I knock once, twice, and a third time, but there's no answer. I decide to see if the door is unlocked, knowing Hunter likes to listen to music while he's working.

The door pops open, and I step inside. Normally, I wouldn't invade his privacy like this, but I feel like I don't have a choice.

I move slowly through the hallway, following the sounds of ... My feet stop just as I round the corner of the hall.

This cannot be happening. *I see Hunter rolling around on the couch with some blonde and hear the sounds of them moaning.*

I can't do this. It was all a big mistake. *I think as I race from his room, leaving the door hanging open behind me.*

"I told you that you didn't want to talk to him right now."

If only I hadn't seen him with another girl, if I'd pushed into the room and told him anyway, or if I'd gone back later. Maybe if I'd been more persistent, or if I hadn't let my own fears of us get in the way…

These dang *what if's* fill my mind constantly.

Things could have been so different if I'd just tried harder. Hannah would know her father. I would still have Hunter.

But then again, things could have still ended up the same. He could have just shaken off the news and kept on living his dream. He could have told me to leave him the hell alone, that he didn't want a daughter or a family.

I want to believe that the choices I made were the right ones. That he would have bailed whether I told him or not.

He's right, though.

I had no way of knowing then or now what would have happened. I made the choice I thought was best at the time.

"I'd like to think I would have come home if you'd told me. I'd like to think things would have been good between us." His words break through my thoughts.

"I'd like to think that too, Hunter, but I'm not so sure. I knew you well enough to know that family and commitment weren't what you wanted at the time. And, honestly, that's what *I* needed then."

It hurts to even think about it, but it's true. He wasn't ready to commit, which was obvious by the fact that he'd left in the first place without saying goodbye.

"Yea I know," he says wistfully. "But what if I can give you that now?"

My eyes open wide with shock. "What do you mean by that?" I ask cautiously.

Surely he doesn't mean commit to *me*.

That's crazy.

We are both so different now. Besides, I hate him.

But even as I think it, I know that's a lie. I don't hate him. Not one bit.

If I weren't so busy trying to hate him, I might actually admit that I still love him.

Maybe.

But probably not.

Because that would be stupid. Who still loves someone who broke their heart?

"I know we can't change the past, Ki, but we can change where our future is going. I meant what I said earlier. I want to know Hannah, and I want to know you again. It seems crazy, but I feel like everything I've been through makes sense now. I still feel like you and I have something, and I'm ready this time if you are." He reaches for my hand and holds it in his.

It feels so good to feel his warmth again, to feel close to him.

My heart races with anticipation, but it shatters just as fast. What happens if he decides this isn't the life he wants again? Will my heart be able to recover a second time if it never really recovered from the first?

"I don't know, Hunter. What if you decide this isn't what you really want? You can walk away, but I don't know if my heart can take it again." A lone tear slides down my cheek, but I don't take my hand from his to wipe it away.

His jaw tightens at my words, and I know he is frustrated, a little angry even. But I can't pretend like the past never happened. I can't let him have my heart again, and I can't let him crush it to pieces when he's done.

Eighteen

Hunter

I understand where Ki is coming from, but damn, if it isn't frustrating as hell for me when we continue to have the same conversation over and over again.

We've gone over what I want so many times at this point, but she still doesn't believe me.

"I don't know what to say to make you trust me, Ki. All I know is that I will try my best to prove to you that I mean what I say."

She looks at me sadly and then turns back out towards the sunset, staying quiet.

I know how she's feeling: tormented by the unknown, by the sudden change.

The colors of the evening sky feel like the different emotions flying between us. Red and orange of anger mixed with some pink for love, blue for clarity, and a hint of white for a clean slate.

A clean slate.

I have the chance to change my life, to make things right, and I intend to do just that.

Ki's soft voice floats through my thoughts. "I'm curious; how do you plan to prove this to me?"

That's a good question, and one I haven't really planned an answer to yet.

But then, a thought comes to me.

"How about we do some things together as a family?"

Ki rolls her eyes. "But we're not a family, Hunter."

"We are a family in every way that counts. Besides, how can I prove to you that I mean it if we don't spend time together?"

We're not a family?

Of course, we're a family. That's my daughter sleeping upstairs. If that doesn't make us a family, then what the hell does?

Marriage?

A ring?

She wants a commitment. A full on, you're the only one for me commitment. And that's what I'm giving her.

Sure, I haven't said those words exactly, but isn't that what I've been getting at?

"Fine," she agrees.

Well, that was easier than I thought it would be.

"Hannah has a game on Saturday morning. Sabrina and Dad are going to hold down the fort at the cafe so I can go. You can come with me if you want?" she says, avoiding my eyes as she brushes her hand through her long hair.

A part of me wishes I could run my fingers through her hair again, too, but she'd probably kill me if I came anywhere near her at the moment.

I shake the crazy thoughts from my head. I cannot go there. Yet.

I have to prove to her that I'm serious, first. Then, maybe I can let myself venture into Ki a little more.

She must be driving me crazy. That's the only way to explain the absolutely ridiculous thoughts going through my mind.

I need to stay focused.

Hannah's soccer game. "I can't think of anything else I'd rather do," I tell her honestly.

She laughs just as the back door opens. Her dad sticks his head out. "Hannah is crying for you."

"Okay, I guess that's my cue." She stands. "Thanks for today. I hope you enjoyed dinner."

She heads into the house before I can say goodbye, and I know it's time for me to leave.

I start down the back porch when the door opens again. I turn, thinking it's Ki, but instead an older, stronger version of her stands in front of me.

She always hated how much she looks like her dad. I wonder if Hannah would hate that about herself too.

I'm not gonna lie, that thought stings a little.

I hadn't seen Ki's dad in five years. The wrinkles around his eyes and across his forehead and the slight brush of gray in his hair show that life had taken its toll on him over the last few years.

"Mr. Carter," I nod. "It's good to see you again, sir." My mom had instilled manners in me as a child, but it's hard to be polite with the look Ki's dad is giving me. It sits somewhere between *I want to kill you* and *I'm glad you're back.*

Personally, I think he's leaning more towards *I want to kill you.*

"Hunter, come sit with me for a minute."

Well shit.

I feel like I know where this talk is going to go. I had the same one with him in high school, even though I'd been friends with Ki since we were kids.

I walk back up the porch steps and sit down in the chair I'd just left. I remain silent, knowing that's what Ki's father expects of me.

I look out at the darkening sky in front of me, the sunset gone along with Ki. There's no mistaking the night rolling in, not in the South. There is nothing to cloud the view as I stare out over the empty land in front of me.

Ki's house is a little more inland, our families not wealthy enough to live in the coastal houses, but we're close enough to still have layers of sand, peeking out through the grass.

That's one thing I love about this place, the fact that you get a little bit of both worlds. You get the beach if you walk over to the south side of town, and you get the grassy fields on the north side.

"I knew you'd come back one day," Mr. Carter states, bringing me back to the present.

"You did?" I blink my eyes at the older man next to me.

How could he possibly know I would come back?

I hadn't even known!

"Don't get me wrong. I didn't want you to come back. Makiya was so upset and heartbroken that first time that I wanted to kill you. Almost went to that University and did right after Hannah was born, but my wife talked me out of it. My crazy, impulsive wife talked me out of doing something crazy and impulsive. It sounds like insanity to admit that." He rocks the chair back and forth, the wooden planks creaking underneath the old, white wooden rocking chair.

I wait for him to continue. "She sat me down that night. She told me that you were going to come back some day, but you needed to come back on your own. She told me that the bond you two had was too strong for you not to. At first, I wasn't so sure, but the more I thought about it, the more I realized she was right. You'd be back someday, and just like me, once you met Hannah, you'd fall in love and never leave. We might be different people, but we both love deeply. I could always see in your eyes how you felt about Ki, even if you didn't realize it."

He looks at me with a clenched jaw and stern eyes. "I am telling you right now, though, that if you hurt my daughter again there will be no other chance. But if you hurt my granddaughter, I will hurt you worse than you could ever imagine. She is my world."

I nod. "I won't hurt them."

"We'll see about that." He stands from the rocking chair and goes back inside. The clanging of the screen door leaving me alone once again.

I make my way to my truck, climb in, and stare at the picture-perfect house in front of me. The grey shingles, black shutters, and intricate front porch make me feel at home.

I had spent so many days and nights at this house as a kid. I had so many fond memories surrounding this place.

Now, I add several more to the log: meeting my daughter, dinner with my family, and a talk that hurt just a little bit if I'm being honest.

I understand where Mr. Carter is coming from - hell, I understand where *everyone* is coming from - but I can't move past the fact that they all think I would hurt my daughter.

Am I really that bad of a person?

I don't think so.

Yea, I've made some mistakes, but I'm not the only one.

You can't make it through life if you don't make a few mistakes.

And if I want to get technical, Ki hadn't told me about my own child. Isn't that considered a mistake?

A big one if you want my opinion.

It doesn't matter though.

The past is in the past, I remind myself. I can't change it.

However, I *will* do everything in my power to be a better man for them, for my family.

It's what they deserve.

Hell, it's what I deserve too.

Nineteen

Makiya

Hunter: I'm outside.

The text flashes across my screen as I pack the last of the snacks into the cooler. I grab my purse, Hannah's bag, and the snacks and sit them next to the front door.

"Hannah, it's time to go!" I yell from the bottom of the stairs.

Within seconds, she stands in front of me with her soccer uniform, pads, and cleats on. "Are you ready?"

She pumps her fist in the air. "Yea, let's go!"

She rushes to the door, opens it, then turns back to me with a grin on her face. "My dad is coming?" she asks when she sees his big truck in the driveway.

I smile back at her. "He sure is."

She squeals as she rushes out the door. I grab the stuff, walk out the door, and lock it behind me.

I feel the bag on my shoulder move and look over to see Hunter trying to take it from me. "Here, let me. Can you grab Hannah's booster seat for my truck though?"

"We can take my car," I suggest.

"Yea, but my truck is a lot nicer than your car," he teases.

He isn't wrong, though. His truck is much nicer and newer than mine. I'd say maybe two years old at the most.

I shake my head and mutter under my breath. "Whatever."

He chuckles as he grabs the rest of the stuff from my arms and heads for the truck.

I pull the booster seat from my car and hand it over to him as well. He sticks it in the backseat like he knows exactly what he's doing, and I find myself wondering where on earth he learned to do that.

Wherever he did, though, I'd like to thank them because it's kind of hot.

After everyone is in the car, we head towards the soccer fields. Heat pumps out of the vents in front of me. It's a cooler spring morning than usual, but it's the perfect temperature for soccer.

At least, as a spectator it is. I'm not sure if it is for those that play - I don't do sports. I'm not coordinated enough.

Once when I was ten, I had the bright idea to play football with Hunter. First pass hit me right in the forehead and I was done.

Hannah has Hunter's talent though. She's very athletic, and graceful too. Thank goodness. I wouldn't wish my lack of ability on anyone.

Soft country music flows from the speakers, and I bob my head up and down to the song. It's a classic, and one of my favorites.

"So, Hannah, are you excited for the game?" Hunter asks her, peering at her through the rearview mirror.

"Yes," she squeals from the backseat.

Squeals have really become her only form of communication, I swear. I wouldn't be surprised if I needed a hearing aid within the next few years. That's how often it occurs.

"Daddy are you really going to watch me play?" she questions, thankfully, without the squeal this time.

She'd been calling him that all morning. *Daddy.* She even told me last night that she thought her dad was pretty cool and she wanted to keep him.

I know Hunter is surprised at her words though. I watch his face as he realizes what she called him. From the passenger seat, I see his eyes quickly well up, and I can't keep the ice from thawing a little bit around my heart.

I'm a sucker for men with children. And men who cry. It's so refreshing to know women aren't the only emotional ones.

He clears his throat, trying to hide the tears. "Yes, I really am. I'm so excited, too."

"Good, because I'm going to be the best today. Just watch."

"I'm sure you will." He wipes a tear from his cheek and smiles at her in the rearview mirror.

I have to admit, he's a hell of a lot sexier to me in this role. There truly is nothing better than watching the man you spent your whole life loving being a dad.

And I have spent my whole life loving him. He was my best friend, my partner in crime. It's only natural that I had fallen for him.

What isn't natural is that I just admitted it now, after everything.

Part of me wanted to take it back the moment it came to mind, but I won't – I can't - because it's the truth.

No matter how much I don't want to admit it, I never stopped loving him. I simply forced the feelings into a vault within my heart.

A vault that, apparently, he had found the code to because I'm way too damn close to letting him open it back up.

Ninety minutes later, Hunter and I sit side by side, watching the game. Hannah kicks the ball down the field, avoiding the other players trying to steal it from her. She stops in front of the net to take her shot, kicking it hard and sending it soaring into the net.

She runs over to us, but instead of coming to me, she goes straight to Hunter.

"Daddy, did you see that?" she yells, jumping up and down in front of him. Clearly, she's making up for all the times she hasn't gotten to say that word.

"I did. You were amazing." She jumps into his arms and gives him a big hug before running back to the field.

I'm shocked by the sudden need for approval from her dad, but I also understand the novelty behind it. She's never had him there before to be proud of her.

Only me.

I sit back and let it happen, knowing it's what my baby girl needs even if I'm completely jealous. Fire is rolling through my stomach and I force myself not to sneer at the scene.

I'm glad she and Hunter hit it off so well. It's almost like he's always been here.

"Does she do that a lot?" Hunter asks, clapping for Hannah as she runs back to the field.

"What? Score a goal?"

"No, come running over when she does?"

I shrug my shoulders, pretending like all of this doesn't bother me. "Not always, but sometimes if she's really excited."

We go back to watching the game. They don't really keep score at this age, but the kids play hard anyway. "You know, Hunter, she came over here because she was excited you got to see it, right?"

The corners of his lips perk up as he leans his head slightly towards me. "Yea?" he asks, seeming excited about it.

"Yea, she hasn't done that to me in a while. She wanted to make sure you were really watching," I mumble, again trying to hide my jealousy.

Damn green monster of envy.

I don't want to be jealous, but I can't help it. It's only ever been me and Hannah. I'm the only one she ever needed approval from. It's going to be hard to get used to this new dynamic we have going on.

"I couldn't take my eyes off of her if I wanted to," he states simply.

"Yea, I know. You haven't taken your eyes off her since the game started."

Maybe I had been wrong this whole time. Maybe he'll turn out to be the best father in the world.

Damn, if that doesn't make me feel even more guilty.

Twenty

Hunter

Watching Hannah play is easily the highlight of my week. My little girl is amazing, and yes, that is my unbiased opinion.

Okay, very biased.

She has so much fight, so much spirit, just like Ki. I have never been prouder of anything in my life, even if I didn't have anything to do with the way she is now.

When the game ends, Hannah comes running towards us, and she latches her arms around my legs. "This is the best day ever."

I have to agree with her.

"How about we go get some lunch?" I ask, looking to Ki to make sure it's okay with her. I may be a part of Hannah's life now, but it's still up to Ki to make the final decision.

She nods, a wide smile on her face. I've always loved her smile. There's something about it that makes you feel cared for, safe.

I've missed seeing that smile aimed at me over the years. Playing college football and winning the championship hadn't meant as much to me as I had thought it would, and that's all because her smiling face hadn't been there with me.

I'll never admit that to her, but it's the truth.

"Yay," Hannah screams excitedly. "Can we go to the diner? I want burgers." She rubs her hand on her tummy like she's starving.

"We absolutely can," I laugh.

We load up our things into the back of the truck and head towards the diner.

Once we're inside, Hannah leads us to the back, stopping in front of the booth by the back window. "Mommy and I sit here every time we come. It's our thing."

"I see. Why's that?"

"Because no one wants to sit back here, we have it all to ourselves," she explains as she slides into the booth.

I let both girls sit down before I slide in next to Hannah. Ki smiles at me from across the table, and I can't help but wonder what's going through her mind right now.

I know what's going through mine: how beautiful she looks, especially in those skintight leggings and long sleeve Southern Girl t-shirt.

An older red headed waitress walks up to our table. I recognize her almost immediately, but not as fast as she recognizes me. "Hunter, is that you?"

"Sure is, Mary Anne. How are you doing?" I stand to give her a hug.

I used to come to the diner all the time in high school, especially after a game. Mary Anne was always my favorite waitress here. She made sure to save a piece of peanut butter pie for me on Friday nights, especially if we won.

"I'm doing well. How about yourself?" she asks, motioning towards everyone at the table.

Before I can respond, she leans in towards Ki and whispers something in her ear. Ki laughs and nods her head, pushing a piece of her hair behind her ear.

That laugh is music to my desperate ears.

I hadn't realized how much I missed Ki until I started spending all my time with her again.

Mary Anne turns back to me, "So, I bet being home is different than you remembered it."

I glance over to Ki and Hannah then back to Mary Anne. "You have no idea."

While we place our order, she and Ki giggle and gossip like old friends.

Once she leaves, I glance around the diner, noting some familiar faces staring back at me. "So, does everyone in town know about Hannah?"

She lifts her shoulders slightly and makes a sneaky face. "Kind of, but you know how it is. It's a small town. Everyone knew she was yours without me saying anything."

"Yea, plus our moms were the biggest gossips in town. I'm sure they blabbed about it as soon as you told them."

Our small town has no secrets, but it doesn't keep the anger from racing through my veins. It's bad enough knowing my mom and Ki kept this gigantic secret from me, but did the whole damn town really have to know, too?

I ball my fists up tightly at my side.

I lived my entire life caring about what this town thought of me. Although, I'm sure the way I destroyed my career destroyed their image of me. I was the golden boy. I highly doubt I still am.

My mom and Ki were right that I've always had bigger dreams and bigger plans than this town could give me, but I also had them because of the people in this town. The people who always showed up to support me on Friday nights, rain or shine.

I can't help but wonder what they think of me now. Do they still think of me the way they had when I was younger?

I wish I didn't care so much about what everyone thinks, but I'm only human. And most humans care about what others think whether they admit it or not.

At least, that's what I tell myself to make me feel better about needing other people's approval. I wish I could not give a shit, like I try to make people think.

"Hunter, I'm sorry," Ki whispers, pulling me from my thoughts.

I sigh and lean back in my seat. Hannah colors a picture on the white paper table mat in front of her. "It's okay, Ki. I'm not mad at you."

"Well, you look pretty pissed off." Of course I'm pissed off, but it doesn't have anything to do with her. It has everything to do with my dumbass self for being such a self-centered idiot.

"Mommy don't say that. You know Jesus don't like those words," Hannah scolds Ki, and I chuckle.

I lean over and nudge Hannah with my shoulder. "You get her girl."

Ki lifts her hand, armed with a paper straw wrapper, and tosses it at me. "Don't encourage her," she shrieks. Then, she looks at Hannah, "I know He doesn't like it when I use those words, but you know Mommy has a bad mouth. Just don't repeat them and everything will be fine."

I bust out laughing again, leaning over the table. I want to call bullshit on her, but I know Hannah will definitely not approve of that word. So, instead I say, "Bullshrimp."

Hannah reaches over with her tiny hands and smacks me on the arm. "What was that for?"

My mouth drops open with shock and Ki leans her head back with laughter. I point at her. "You think this is funny? She just hit me."

"Yea, and if you do it again, she'll hit you again. I told you, she's all me, and trust me when I say, it's hard to punish the *you* in your child," she laughs.

I look down at Hannah who continues to color like nothing happened. "Hannah, you can't hit your father."

"You said a bad word," she says like it explains everything.

"Bullshrimp isn't a bad word," I argue with the five-year-old version of Ki.

What the hell is wrong with me? I'm not going to win this argument. It's a mini-Ki sitting next to me.

A fiery, stubborn, independent, and way wiser than her years mini-Ki.

"Daddy, Gramma says that just because we change the word doesn't mean we change the invention." I feel a pang in my heart when she mentions my mom.

"Intention, honey," Ki pipes up from across the table.

Oh, so, now she steps into the conversation.

"Anyway, Gramma says God still knows the word was meant to be bad," Hannah says, looking at both of us with wide, insistent eyes.

I mean I definitely can't argue with that, but I can have a chat with my foul-mouthed mother.

"Well, I think Daddy needs to have a talk with Gramma about this." I look at Ki who's trying desperately not to laugh again but is failing miserably.

"Good luck," she mutters from across the table.

Hannah shrugs. "She's gonna tell you what I just told you."

And I know she will, but I also know the kind of colorful vocabulary my mom uses when she's angry.

A little while later, I pull into Ki's driveway and park my truck. I reach for the door handle, but Ki stops me, placing her hand on my arm. It feels like an electric shock through my bloodstream.

I can't believe she still has this effect on me after all these years.

"Thank you for today," she whispers, trying not to wake Hannah who fell asleep on the ride back.

"No, thank you," I insist because I mean it.

She has no idea how much this day meant to me.

She gazes out the front window of my black Silverado. I want to know what she's thinking, but I figure it's pretty serious, considering how tight her jaw is and how tense her shoulders look. "You okay, Ki?"

She nods slowly, continuing to gaze out the window. After a few more beats of silence, she faces me. "I'm glad you came back. I think Hannah needs you more than I'd like to admit. She was so happy today, and it made everything worth it."

Okay. That's definitely the last thing I expect to hear come out of Ki's mouth, but I'm glad she said it.

I reach for Ki across the console. It pokes me in the side, making me a little uncomfortable, but I push through the awkward pain.

I wrap my arms around her, giving her a lopsided hug. I don't know if she wants one, but I need it. My heart beats faster as she leans into me the best she can over the middle.

We both laugh as we separate from each other. "Probably would have been a better idea to get out of the car and give you a hug, but I needed that."

Her smile puts a twinkle in her eyes.

Or maybe I do.

"I'm glad you did. Hunter, I know I don't show it, and I'm sorry for that, but I really am happy you're back." She averts her eyes and rubs her hands together, fidgeting in nervousness. "I'm just scared."

I grab her hands and close them in mine. They are half my size, but they still fit perfectly.

"Honestly, I am too. But I promise that I won't intentionally hurt you. I'm not walking away this time, at least not without a fight." I squeeze her hands softly.

Her lips curve into a small smile, lighting up her brown eyes even more. I could look at her forever and never get tired of it.

I let go of her hands and reach for the door handle again. "Should we get Hannah inside?"

"Yea, probably. You want to carry Hannah in while I grab everything else?"

"Absolutely," I say, practically jumping out of the truck.

There's no way in hell I'm passing that up.

Twenty-One
Makiya

I knead my fingers in the dough I'm prepping for tomorrow morning's rush. I'm sure I look like a complete mess, especially if the flour across my shirt and apron are any indication.

This entire week has been a blur. The cafe has been slam packed every day, and both Hannah and Hunter have kept me on my toes.

I laugh softly. Even if the week has gone by crazy fast, it's been a great week.

"Hey," Sabrina says, slapping her hands down on the table in front of me. "If you knead that dough anymore, the bread will taste like your dang fingers."

"Aren't you supposed to be out front manning the register?" I ask, glancing up at her.

"Yea, sure, if there were any customers left, but it's three in the afternoon. Ya know, closing time for us."

"It's three already?" I ask, looking over at the basic clock hanging over the doorway.

"Sure is, and ya know what that means?" Sabrina's eyes light up and a sneaky grin dances across her face. "Party time starts in a few hours," she squeals.

I look at her like she's an idiot. "Party time? Really? Coming from the girl who passed out before eight at the last girls night."

She crosses her arms in front of her, pouting. "That's only because you made me open that day so you could get your damn beauty rest."

"Yea, yea, excuses, excuses," I taunt, trying to hide my smile.

She laughs. "I'll see ya at 6. And don't be late."

"When have you ever known me to be late?" I holler after her as she heads to leave.

"There's a first time for everything," she yells over her shoulder.

She's not wrong, but I'm also never late.

I finish up the preparations for tomorrow, wrapping the dough up and placing it to the side, then, head out for the night.

A few hours later I pull up to Sabrina's apartment building, noting London just pulling in. I get out of my car and wave as she gets out of her car.

"So, you found someone to watch Brayden for the night?" I holler at her as we both make our way towards the entrance.

"Yea, he went to a sleepover at one of his friends' houses. Thank goodness! I was going to cry if I didn't get a girls' night soon." London says bringing me into a hug once we're closer together.

I'd be jealous of London if I didn't know her so well. She's gorgeous, with curves most women dream of having and exceptional blue eyes.

I had known London most of my life, even though she was a few years older than me. It *is* a small town after all.

"I hear ya," I say, continuing up the two flights of stairs to Sabrina's apartment.

"So, who's watching Hannah tonight?" London asks as we stop just in front of apartment 304.

"Hunter," I answer, slightly out of breath thanks to my lack of activity over the last few years. Although, it could be my nerves from knowing these girls are about to grill me on all things Hunter.

"Ah," London hums, a sneaky smile curling the ends of her lips.

Before I can ask her what the look means, Sabrina swings the door open. "Hey girls!" she squeals, holding a large glass of red wine.

"Looks like you started the party without us," I laugh, stepping into Sabrina's house. I leave my shoes by the door and join her at the large bar-like table in her dining area.

"Yea, you couldn't wait until we got here?" London asks, sitting down between us.

"Y'all were taking your sweet ole time, so ya know, I decided to pregame," Sabrina shouts, pumping her glass into the air.

"What are we, in college?" I giggle. Out of all three of us, Sabrina is the craziest. She's impulsive, wild, and does a lot of dumb shit, but she's got a huge heart. She's the one you want in your corner when everything is falling apart.

"Anyway," Sabrina starts, shimmying her eyebrows up and down at me. "Tell us about Hunter. How are things?" She speaks so slowly, making sure to emphasize each word suggestively.

"Fine," I mutter, pouring myself the largest glass of wine possible. I'm beyond grateful that my best friend owns the biggest wine glasses known to man.

"Seriously, that's all you got?" Her attitude makes her Southern drawl come out even thicker.

London puts her finger up as she sips on her wine. "Actually, I'd say things are going really well, considering Hunter is watching Hannah tonight."

Sabrina peers at me with wide eyes. I roll my eyes and chug half the glass of wine. I'm going to need ten times this amount if I'm going to make it through the rest of this conversation. "He's her dad," I state, defensively. "I mean I can't exactly keep him from her."

"Or from yourself?" Sabrina waves her hand nonchalantly in the air, finishing off the last of her wine already.

"It's not like that," I argue, knowing it's pointless. It doesn't matter what I say, Sabrina isn't going to believe me.

I mean is it nice having him around? Yea, sure. Would it be nice if it could last? Absolutely. But I'm not an idiot, I'm a realist.

At least, that's what I tell myself.

"It's never like that," London adds. "But it always becomes that, just wait and see."

I glance between them and sigh. "Maybe for some people, but not for me."

"You say that now," Sabrina snorts.

"Do you still love him?" London questions, peering over her glass of wine at me.

"Uh," I hesitate. I don't have any idea how to answer this that won't make these girls crazy.

I want to say no because that's the rational answer. Who still loves their ex after they broke their heart? But I also know that rational is a complete lie. Nothing about any of this is rational or realistic.

"I knew it," Sabrina smirks. "You gave it away when you gave him the job."

"I did that because we needed the help," I huff.

Sabrina points to London. "But you could have asked London to help."

London puts her hands up in the air, defensively. "Now, now, ya know I've got too much on my plate already."

"Yea, what she said," I point my thumb at London.

Sabrina chuckles and lifts her glass to the air once more. "Here's to pretending we don't have feelings for our exes."

I roll my eyes again, but I raise my glass anyway. There might just be some truth to her words after all.

Twenty-Two

Hunter

I'm not freaking out.

I'm not sweating in places I didn't even know you could sweat.

I'm perfectly fine.

Except I'm not. I'm freaking the fuck out.

It's my first time alone with my daughter, and I don't have any fucking clue what to do.

Does she wear diapers or does she potty on the toilet? What the hell does she eat? Do I need to block her in a room on her own so she doesn't get hurt? Shouldn't there be locks on the cabinets?

I know I'm being completely irrational at the moment. I've spent enough time with Hannah to know she can take care of herself for the most part.

I also know she doesn't wear diapers or need locked in a room, but I feel like I've lost all sense tonight.

But, hell, I don't want to fuck this up.

Why did my parents and Ki think it was a good idea to leave Hannah with me alone for the evening?

I take a deep breath and face the one thing in this life that scares me the most – my daughter.

She looks at me, her face scrunched like I'm crazy. I mean she's not far off. I'm pretty sure I've lost my damn mind tonight.

"Are you okay?" she questions, frowning slightly.

"Yea," I respond, brushing off all the ridiculous nerves coursing through my body.

I've got this. I'm a man for fuck's sake. I can definitely handle this.

"You look like you're not okay," she states.

I'm nowhere near okay. But this is my child, and I will figure it out. I mean that's what parents do. I think?

"I'm fine," I say, firmly. "So, what do you want to do tonight?"

She shrugs her shoulders as she runs her fingers along the grains of wood on the table. "I don't know," she mutters.

I sit down beside her and cross my arms on the table, bringing myself to her level. "Well, what do you usually do with your mom?"

A smile lifts the corner of her lips. "We usually play dress-up. Mommy lets me do her hair and make-up." A frown slowly forms on her face. "But you won't want to do that," she mumbles, looking so sad it breaks my heart.

"Why wouldn't I?"

Her familiar eyes meet mine. "Because daddies don't like to play dress-up."

"And who told you that?"

"The TV," she says, so naturally.

"Well, maybe some daddies don't, but this daddy does." I point my thumb at my chest and feel an overwhelming sensation flood my heart when she grins.

She jumps out of her chair and runs over to the bright pink backpack she brought with her. She pulls out what looks like a make-up bag, some frilly hair things, and a big feathery scarf.

What the hell did I just agree to?

She brings all the items over to where I sit, dropping them on the table. Then, she pulls the chair up to me. "Turn so I can see you."

I do as I'm told, regretting more and more to agreeing to this every passing minute.

She climbs onto the chair and begins the process, telling me what she's going to do each step of the way.

She giggles when she accidentally puts lipstick on my cheek and squeals when I shake my head as she's trying to put a clip in my hair.

When she's done, she hands me a mirror and shrieks excitedly, "You look beautiful. Do you like it?"

I hold the mirror up to my face and note the bright blue eye shadow around my eyes, red lipstick that's nowhere near my actual lips, and the too light powdery stuff covering my face.

I swallow hard, put on my best smile, and choke out, "I love it."

"Yay," she yells.

"Hey, what's all the …," Riley pauses just inside the kitchen. "What the hell happened to your face?" he asks, holding back a laugh, which I know is for Hannah's sake and not mine.

"Uncle Riley, you said a bad word," Hannah chastises.

Riley puts a hand to his chest. "I'm so sorry, Hannah," he apologizes, dramatically.

She giggles and points to my face. "You're forgiven. Do you like his face? I did it all by myself," she exclaims, proudly.

Riley walks over to us and kneels in front of Hannah, smiling. "It's beautiful. I love it."

He turns to me. "And how does Dad like it?"

"I think she did a great job."

Riley chuckles and stands. "Mom told me you were here alone with Hannah. I thought I'd come check in on you." He points to Hannah. "But I think you've got everything covered."

"Can I go watch some TV?" Hannah asks, jumping up from her chair and putting her things away, clearly bored with the adult conversation.

"Sure, princess," I respond, making her smile.

Once she's packed up her stuff, she runs down the hall to the living room. I hear the faint sound of the TV and sigh. "All I've done is sit here while she put makeup on me, but damn, I feel exhausted."

"That's because they have so much energy. We don't even have to move; their energy just makes us tired." Riley speaks, taking the seat across from me and wiping some leftover make-up off the table.

"Yea, I see that. You learn that from watching Hannah?"

He nods, cautiously. "Yea, I've watched her for Ki a few times over the years, and of course, when Mom's had her, we've spent time together."

A pang of jealousy hits me hard in the gut. My brother has spent more time with my daughter than me.

I should have expected it considering Ki didn't keep it a secret from my family, but still, this hits a little differently.

I can't say why, it just does.

"I'm sorry," Riley mutters, staring down at his hands. My usually happy, go lucky brother looks somber and sad.

I sigh deeply, knowing none of this is his fault. "You don't need to be. I mean none of this makes any sense to me, but I've decided it's best to just accept it and move on. It's not like I can do a damn thing about it anyway."

"I get that, but it still wasn't fucking right to do that to you. You have every right to be pissed beyond belief at me, Mom, Dad shit, all of us."

"Maybe but being pissed doesn't change a damn thing."

And it doesn't.

Neither does being jealous of every single person who got to know Hannah when I didn't.

Twenty-Three

Makiya

Every day that passes, I'm still surprised to see Hunter showing up each morning to work at the café, texting me every day, and spending his free time with me and Hannah.

Am I happy? Yes.

But maybe a little terrified too.

Because every day that he shows up means I'm another day closer to dropping the protective barriers around my heart.

Of course, after hearing about his night alone with Hannah (because Hannah has talked about it for the last five days straight), the barriers started coming down a little faster.

I hand a receipt to the customer in line and go to make their coffee and wrap up their pastry. It's almost closing time and thankfully there aren't many people left in the shop.

Soft country music plays from the radio in the back, and I bob my head to the beat. We always play the older classic country music, none of that new country music that verges on pop.

That's just how it is down in the south. It's the only music I've ever listened to. It was also my mom's favorite. She always had it playing in the café, and I can't bear to change the station, so I leave it.

These are my favorite times of the day. The customers slowly pour out and the satisfaction of another good day lingers in the air.

When I first started working in the café, I had my doubts about my abilities. I told my mom she was crazy for thinking I could handle everything.

Then, my mom got sick. Everything about the cafe landed on my shoulders, completely overwhelming me.

That's when I realized my anxiety was a real problem. The doctor told me therapy would be the best option. So, I tried it, but talking about it only made me obsess more.

After six months, the therapist recommended a small dose of medication to help take the edge off. It worked, and it became easier for me to accept the things I couldn't control. Now, the anxieties of the café have given way to the love I have for it.

Running the cafe had never been my passion, not until I had no choice. In the days my mother was battling cancer, I found that I had a real knack for baking and cooking. I came up with my own recipes to add to the menu and they had been successful.

That's when my feelings towards the café changed, and I realized that I loved the place as much as my mom did.

Some of those items are still on the menu now. My bestsellers, actually.

Days like today are when I miss my mom the most.

My mom had always been my confidant when it came to boys or love or really anything for that matter. There's nothing I wouldn't give to be able to talk to her about everything going on. I know she would have had some crazy opinions about Hunter being back.

But she isn't here. All I have is my dad, and as much as I love my dad, he's a crazy redneck.

Kind of like me.

Once, he tried to pull a gun on a boy who came over to study with me. He thought he was trying to "get some" because he was sitting too close. An unfortunately true story.

He even took me out that day to the shooting range just to make sure I still remembered how to use a gun. Told me one day I might need it.

I know my dad just wants to protect me from everything, but my mom had always wanted me to experience things for myself. She'd always encouraged me to follow my heart.

I know that's what she would tell me to do now, but I don't want to trust my heart. I had trusted it five years ago, and it was wrong. I'm so afraid that maybe I'm the problem.

Maybe I'm just unlovable.

It just hasn't seemed like it's in the cards for me.

Then, Hunter walks through the door of the café holding Hannah's hand, breaking into my thoughts. I try to ignore the sudden leap in my chest and the whirlwind of fear, anxiety, and joy that run through me.

"Hey, you two!" I squat down to give Hannah a hug. "How was school today?"

"It was great! Ms. Valentine told Daddy she liked him," she blurts out in excitement, looking at Hunter with a devious smirk.

Yea, definitely not in the cards for me.

I act like I'm not jealous with a smirk of my own, but truthfully, I'm so jealous that I want to go find Ms. Valentine and give her a great big knuckle sandwich.

"Is that right?" I lift my eyebrow and glance up at Hunter.

I really hope he doesn't catch onto the shade of green I've suddenly turned.

"That's right," Hannah says. "Momma, I'm hungry. Can I have a biscuit and jam?" she yells, running behind me and to the kitchen before I can answer.

"Just be careful," I respond back loudly as I hear clanging in the kitchen.

I'm sure there will be a big mess to clean up later, but Hannah is exceptionally independent. Even if I try to help, she'll just kick me out anyway.

Hunter tips his head toward the back of the café. "Will she be okay in there by herself?"

"Yea, she'll be fine. I put all the things she shouldn't get into out of reach for a reason," I say, putting my hands on my waist. "Now, tell me more about Ms. Valentine."

My damn jealousy makes me seem way more interested than I am.

Even if deep down I'm dying to know more.

He puts his hands up in the air in defense. "Okay, so clearly, it's not how Hannah made it sound."

"Uh-huh."

He shakes his head at me and chuckles. "Okay, fine, she hit on me when I walked to the front of the school to pick up Hannah."

"And?"

He scrunches his eyebrows together and frowns. "Are you jealous, Ki?"

I shrug off his question. "No."

He laughs off my lie. "Nice try, but I know you're lying."

Dang it! I knew there was a reason I hated him. He'd always been able to tell when I wasn't telling the truth, a perk of knowing someone so well. A curse, really, depending on how you look at it.

Frankly, I'm leaning towards curse at the moment.

He lays his hands on my shoulders. "Ki, I'm here because of you. I promise I brushed it off and told her I wasn't single."

Well, that surprises me.

"You told her you weren't single?" I kick my feet across the floor, pretending I don't really care about the answer.

But I do. I so care.

His finger lifts my chin up to look him in the eyes. "Are *you* single?"

"We never really discussed what we were." It's a ploy to get him off the jealousy track, but it's also the truth.

"No, I guess we didn't," he sighs and pulls me closer. "So, let's talk about it now. I stayed because I want us to be a family. That means I want you and Hannah, not one or the other. Understand?"

My heart nearly beats out of my chest. "Yes."

"That also means that we are, as of today, in a relationship, so if you have any men out there you were stringing along, you need to dump 'em. Now," he demands, and dang, if that doesn't turn me on just a little.

I roll my eyes at his blatant stupidity and cough out a laugh.

Me? Stringing along guys?

Not likely.

"We both know that isn't the case," I say.

A huge grin spreads across his face as he winks. "Just checking."

"Whatever." I shove him a bit as I slide past him to go check on Hannah.

"So, it's a deal? We're a couple." I cringe as he yells it across the café.

"I guess it has to be considering you just told the entire town," I respond a little quieter, but still loud enough for everyone to hear.

It's not like the café is packed at the moment, but gossip travels fast in Sunrise.

All you need is one nosy body to make it in the town grapevine.

And that's exactly what I want to avoid: being part of the town gossip.

Twenty-Four

Hunter

I can't believe Ki is jealous of Ms. Valentine.

She's definitely not my type.

I have one type, and she's currently sitting in front of me, talking to my mom.

I never knew Ki to be the jealous type, but obviously I had been wrong. From the look on her face, the green monster had taken over the minute Hannah spilled the beans.

I think it's hilarious; I assumed when I told her I wanted to be there for her, she knew I meant as more than just friends.

Clearly, I need to be more specific with things when it comes to Ki.

Women.

I'm even more surprised that she agreed to be my girlfriend.

Technically, we hadn't used those exact words, but that's what she is to me. Even if she isn't too keen on giving me a second chance just yet.

"I'm so glad you girls stopped by this evening. I'm sorry I didn't have any dinner left," my mom says beside me.

My mom was so excited when I came home and told her Ki and Hannah were coming over. I think I even saw the hint of a tear in her eye when I told her.

I know she wants me to have a chance to make things right, and that she feels guilty for her part in keeping Hannah from me.

"It's okay, Rose. We ate already anyway. Hannah just wanted to come visit with you," Ki explains.

"You girls are more than welcome over here anytime."

They continue to discuss Hannah and how things are going while I contemplate the best way to ask Ki to be my date to my brother's wedding.

I know she's invited, she told me that already, but she hadn't said if she was going or not.

We haven't talked much about it or anything other than Hannah, really. That seems to be the way Ki wants it, and I'm trying to follow her lead.

It's hard, though.

I'm not really a follow the leader kind of guy. Never have been, but I'm trying to do things differently this time around.

I want nothing more than to show the whole town and our families that Ki is mine, but I don't think she'd like that.

Yet.

That's why I want her to be my date to my brother's wedding. One, I can show her off to the entire town and my family. Two, I can have some alone time with her after.

And I have the perfect plan set up.

"How about some dessert?" Mom pipes up, standing and forcing me out of my thoughts.

Hannah squeals from the chair next to me as she sees my mom pull the ice cream and toppings out. "You like ice cream I see?"

She puts her hands on her hips and pouts her lips. "I don't *like* ice cream. I *looooooove* ice cream."

My five-year-old child has more attitude than any teenage girl and that terrifies the shit out of me.

What the hell is she going to be like when she hits fifteen?

"Well good thing I love ice cream, too!" I tickle her softly, knocking the attitude from her face. She giggles and squirms, trying to get away.

"Daddy, stop, that tickles," she squeaks out between laughs.

I glance to my mom preparing the dessert. Her body freezes in time, and I know exactly what she's thinking and feeling. It's how I felt when Hannah first called me dad.

Mom reaches a finger up to her eye and swipes away a few loose tears.

Ki stands and walks over to my mom. She whispers something in her ear and Mom smiles at her, and then they hug each other.

Mom looks as though she doesn't want to let go, but she steps back slowly, wiping a few more renegade tears away.

She and Ki bring some bowls of ice cream to the table and a variety of toppings: sprinkles, chocolate syrup, maraschino cherries, whipped cream, and a few other things I pay no attention to.

"First, you put the whipped cream on," Hannah explains to me as she squirts whipped cream on the top of her ice cream. "Then, you put some chocolate syrup and sprinkles. Last, you put the cherry on the top. Right, Gramma?" She looks to my mom for approval.

She's right. It's how my mom taught all of us to make sundaes when we were younger. I can't believe she carried the tradition on with Hannah.

My mom scoops a bit of her sundae into her mouth and nods. "That's right baby girl. Then, we eat."

Hannah picks up a huge scoop of ice cream. "You think you can fit all that in your mouth?" I ask her. She stops to study the spoon for a moment.

Then, she looks at me sideways. "Can you?"

I twist my lips in thought. "Hm, I don't know. Should we see?"

Her eyes light up as she yells "Yes!" a little too loud.

"Hannah, inside voice, remember?" Ki prompts from the other side of the table.

Hannah covers her mouth as she giggles. "Oops, sorry."

Ki grins at her. "It's okay, baby."

Hannah looks at me and points to my bowl. "Get as big a bite as you can." I scoop up the biggest bite I can fit on my spoon, which is twice the size of Hannah's. "When I say go, eat it! Ready, set, go!" she screeches before shoveling the ice cream into her mouth.

She gets more ice cream and whipped cream on her nose and face than in her mouth, and I get the worst brain freeze of my life.

Clearly, I hadn't thought this one through all the way.

I put my tongue to the roof of my mouth as I squish my face together, trying to ward off the cold coursing through my brain.

Hannah laughs hard next to me. She holds her belly as she giggles until she can't breathe anymore. "Got you!" she yells.

I tilt my head to the side and crinkle my brows together. "You got me?"

"Yea, I put all the whipped cream on my spoon, see?" She shows me her bowl.

Well, what do you know, my kid is smart as hell. "But you put a lot of ice cream on yours."

I laugh along with her. "You sure did get me. I should have thought of that one."

She shrugs her shoulders. "We can't all be smart."

My eyes widen with shock. I glance over to Ki and her eyes twinkle with laughter. "You taught her that one, didn't you?"

She puts her palms up in the air. "I say it a lot, but I didn't know she was paying attention."

"Yea, sure," I say, not entirely convinced.

Actually, I'm almost one hundred percent positive that Ki taught her that phrase on purpose and showed her how to use it against me just because she can.

It's something younger Ki would have done, so I'm pretty sure older Ki would do the same.

"Believe what you want," Ki pretends not to care, but the sexy smirk she wears says otherwise.

"Well, I'm going to let you three spend some time together." My mom stands and gathers all the bowls from the table.

"Mom, you don't need to leave. Ki and Hannah came to see you." She looks at me, a knowing smile on her face.

She quirks one eyebrow up as if to say they hadn't come to visit her. They had come to spend time with me.

I frown slightly. I feel bad for making her feel like she has to run off.

"It's okay. There's a bath calling my name upstairs, and I think I'm going to have to answer it."

A crease forms between Hannah's brows and her nose wrinkles up. "Gramma, I don't hear anything calling your name."

I try to hold a straight face, but I bust out laughing as Ki and my mom do the same.

Hannah glances around the room, more confused now than she had been before.

I gently lay my hand on her shoulder. "Gramma didn't mean it was literally calling her name. It was a metaphor."

"What's a me-ta-for?"

"It means Gramma really wants to take a bath," I explain, brushing a lock of red hair from her face.

Her nose wrinkles up a little more. "Well why didn't she just say that?"

I turn my gaze to my mom and snicker. "That's a good question, Hannah. I think it's because Gramma is weird."

Hannah's giggles are music to my ears until my mom's hand whips me upside the head. "Just remember Hunter, you still live under my roof." She smirks as she saunters out of the room.

Twenty-Five

Makiya

I stare at Hunter's fine ass - I mean butt - as I follow him outside to my car.

I'm completely amazed at how good he still looks after all this time. I can't count how many times I'd thought about him over the last few weeks or how many times I'd had some very naughty dreams with him as the star.

I can't blame myself for it.

It's not like I'd acted on them.

Yet.

It's been so long since I'd felt this way about anyone or even remotely thought about having sex like this. I mean I haven't been celibate or anything the last five years, but I haven't exactly gone on a dating spree either.

It's crazy how quickly my feelings for Hunter fired back up.

It doesn't help that he continues to show up and follow through. How can I ignore that?

Hannah has literally consumed the last five years of my life. I would never change that, either. She's the best part of my life.

Hunter stops as he reaches the front of my car. Hannah stands beside him, holding onto his hand.

I love how attached she's become to him in such a short amount of time. It also terrifies me.

But, that's Hannah for you.

She's fiercely independent and falls in love so fast. That's one reason I never really dated anyone. I couldn't stand to break her heart, too.

Him being here for her is a good thing, no matter my own feelings about it. She needs her dad. Just like I need him.

The moment the thought enters my mind, I shake it out.

I do *not* need him.

At least, I don't think so.

"Thank you for coming over tonight," he says as I stop in front of him.

"Thank you for suggesting it. I haven't brought Hannah over since before you came back because I wasn't sure it was a good idea or what you wanted."

"I think it was good for mom to see you two and me together." Hannah lifts her arms to Hunter, and he picks her up, pulling her close to his chest.

"Also, I forgot to tell you earlier because you were so jealous," he pauses with a smirk on his face. "They're having a Spring Fair for families on Thursday night at the school. I thought maybe we could take Hannah."

"I think that would be a great idea."

We make a plan, and then he quietly suggests we get Hannah in the car before she falls asleep in his arms. He buckles her in and kisses her on the forehead before whispering, "I love you, princess."

She mutters back, "I love you, too."

His words thaw my heart a tiny bit more. It sounds cliché, but it's true. If he keeps it up, my heart will eventually be mush around him again.

I'm not sure if that's good or bad.

Hunter shuts the door and turns to me. "I wanted to ask you something." He steps towards me until we're only a few inches apart.

"Okay?" I whisper, a little nervous.

"Would you and Hannah be my date for my brother's wedding this weekend? I don't know if you were planning on going, but I really want you both to go with me."

"Hunter," I sigh.

I really, really want to say yes, but I'm not sure it's a good idea. Am I ready to take the next step, to pronounce "us" officially to everyone?

Although, technically, we'd already done that. Mary Anne would have told half the town after we left the diner the other night. And the other half would have found out because Hunter practically screamed it to the world in the café earlier today.

"Look, I know it's a lot all at once, especially after everything I did to you, but I really want you to be there with me. I want to show you and Hannah off to everyone. Plus, it wouldn't feel right if you weren't there."

I understand where he's coming from.

Truthfully, it sounds amazing to me. It's all I've ever wanted from him, but I feel like all of this is too good to be true.

In my mind, I hear my dad telling me Hunter deserves the chance, mom saying to follow my heart.

So, I do.

"Yes, okay, we will go with you."

"Great!" he says so loudly that the next-door neighbor peeks her aged and wrinkled face through the front window.

"Looks like Mrs. Poniatowski isn't as excited about it as you are." I point my head towards her window.

Hunter waves her off. "She'll get over it when she finds out why I was so loud."

I reach to open my car door. "Well, I should be going. It's been a long day and Hannah has school tomorrow."

"You don't have to lie to me Ki. I know it's way past your bedtime," he teases.

And, yea, it kind of is past my bedtime. If the sun's asleep, I'm asleep.

I smack him playfully on the arm. "Oh, shut up."

I like that we had fallen so easily back into a rhythm. Our whole lives had consisted of teasing each other, telling each other everything, and making sure the other didn't get too big of an ego.

The last part more for Hunter than myself.

I don't want to say we complete each other because that's too cliché, but we kind of do. Our personalities complement each other. We just *work* together.

Hunter hooks his arm around my neck and pulls me in close. It feels so good to be in his arms again. I lay my head on his shoulder and wrap my arms around his large frame. I've missed him.

I'll admit it.

I had really, really missed him.

"It feels so good to have you in my arms again," he mutters next to my ear, sending shivers down my spine. He has no idea just how good it feels for me, too.

I lean my head back to look at his face. His chiseled features have always made me jealous. He is the perfect specimen. His crooked jaw is covered with a thick beard, not too full, but not too trim either. It's just the way I like it.

Yes, I'm a sucker for beards. Take it up with the women of the South, it's kind of our thing.

His eyes search mine frantically for permission. I know what he wants to do. It's the same thing I want, but I'm so afraid.

Of everything that could possibly happen.

Anxiety seriously ruins everything.

When I make no move to respond, he speaks softly, "I really want to kiss you."

"I know, but -" He stops me with a touch of his finger to my lips.

Did he really just shush me?

I'm about to give him a piece of my mind when he says, "Let's not worry about the future. Let's worry about you and me, right here, right now, okay?"

I can't form any argument or coherent words when he makes so much sense.

When did he become so philosophical?

He leans forward, his lips touching mine.

The kiss is gentle at first. Sweet. Romantic even.

Then, he brushes his tongue along my lips, and I open up for him with a small moan.

Gah, it feels so good.

Our tongues lash against each other as the kiss becomes stronger and more aggressive. Need surges through me.

I move closer to him. I feel his hard on against my leg and it turns me on even more. It's a damn shame that Hannah is in the car beside us.

Our lips mold together for one last round before I pull back slowly.

His chest rises and falls as he tries to catch his breath.

"That. Was. Amazing," he says, emphasizing each word as he holds my face between his two hands.

"It was beyond amazing," I agree.

He dips his head for one last chaste kiss before he steps back. "As much as I would love to keep this going, our daughter is waiting in the car for you to take her home." His hands rub circles on my waist. I don't want him to let go, but he's right. Hannah needs to go to bed.

I step out of his embrace, watching his hands fall to his side. "Yea, I should get her home."

I climb in the driver's seat and start the car. He lays his hand on the top of the door and bends towards me. "We *will* continue this later. You can count on that." He presses his lips to my cheek and then shuts my door.

I have no doubts we will be continuing that later.

In fact, I'm pretty sure if I'm given the chance, there will be a lot more than kissing going on.

Twenty-Six

Hunter

The kiss between me and Ki had driven me crazy the entire night. My mind kept flinging images of her doing some very naughty things to me while I tried to sleep.

Which explains why I was so horny when I woke up.

The kiss had been incredible, way better than any kiss in high school or any after Ki. It had taken on a life of its own without me even realizing it, and I hadn't wanted it to end.

As I stand just inside the back door of the cafe, watching Ki get everything ready for the day, I know it'll be painfully hard for me to not spend all day with my lips on hers, but I don't have much of a choice.

She looks amazing in her skintight, straight-legged jeans, perfectly emphasizing her pert ass, and a purple top that shows just enough cleavage to tease me.

"Good morning," I announce as I saunter up to her with a daring smirk on my face.

She blushes, a light shade of pink coloring her cheeks. "Morning, Hunter. You know you don't have to keep coming in so early. You're just working on the business stuff, so you can come in later."

At least I'm not the only one who was affected by that damn kiss.

I stop just in front of her and put my hands on both her hips. Her cheeks darken a deeper shade of pink.

Yea, that kiss definitely affected her as much as it did me.

I can't begin to describe the pleasure that brings me either.

"But then, I wouldn't be able to do this." I turn her face to meet mine and push my lips against hers. I keep the kiss short and sweet, knowing Sabrina will be here any minute to start opening up.

As we part, she smiles. "You know what I change my mind. You definitely need to be here early. In fact, you should probably start coming in even earlier."

I chuckle. "Of course, you think that now. Too bad, you already told me I could come in later so you can expect me here at nine tomorrow." I kiss her one more time before heading to the back office.

Sabrina arrives not too long after, and I'm glad I'm in the office when she does arrive.

The minute she walks in, she screeches, "Explain, right now!"

I should get up to shut the door, but I really want to know exactly *what* Ki needs to explain to her. I stay as quiet as I can while I listen, with only a bit of guilt.

It's not like Ki will ever know.

"There's nothing to explain," Ki speaks softly, trying to keep me from hearing but failing. The kitchen echoes way more than she thinks.

"Of course, there is! You sent me a text saying, '*We kissed.*' And that was it. Nothing else."

"And?"

I hear a thud, and I imagine Sabrina stomping her foot in frustration and slamming her fists onto her hips. "No, you are not getting off that easy. As your best friend, I insist that you tell me every detail that happened between you and Hunter. At least, I assume it was Hunter; you didn't clarify that either."

Even though I know it's me they're talking about, Sabrina's statement sends a spurt of rage and jealousy through my veins, making the muscles in my back tense.

I could be wrong.

Ki could have met up with another guy after she left my mom's house.

I take a deep breath, trying to cool down and remind myself that Ki was with *me* last night.

"Sabrina," Ki whines, clearly not wanting to explain anymore to her.

A soft tapping begins, and I know it's Sabrina waiting impatiently for Ki to answer.

The good thing about knowing both of them so well is that I can picture their actions without actually seeing them do it. It's kind of like watching a movie in my head.

"Fine," Ki finally gives in. "I'll tell you, but only because I know you won't leave it alone until I do, and we open in thirty minutes."

"Thank you, now proceed."

"We went over to visit Rose last night, with Hunter obviously, and had a great time eating ice cream and catching up. Then, Hunter walked us out to the car. He put Hannah in the car, and we started talking. He asked me to go to Riley's wedding with him, then, he sort of kissed me."

Ki barely stops talking before Sabrina starts with a million questions. "First off, he asked you to go with him to the wedding?"

"Yes."

"And what did you say?"

"I said yes."

"Then, he *sort of* kissed you?"

"Uh-huh."

"How does one *sort of* kiss? Like he half-touched your lips, half-didn't? Or like, you don't want to tell me about the kiss because it was amazingly earth-shattering so you're saying sort of?"

"Um…" Ki trails off.

Sabrina giggles. "I knew it. It was an amazingly earth-shattering kiss!"

"I thought you'd be upset about it," Ki mumbles.

"Upset?" Sabrina asks. "Hell no! I mean when he first got back, I wanted to kick him in the balls, but you seem happy. He's different, and I want you two to work things out. You've always been perfect for each other. He just needs to see that, too."

I picture Ki chewing on her bottom lip and send myself into a sex-driven frenzy while I wait for her to say something. "You don't think I gave in too quickly?"

"It doesn't matter what I think, Ki. What matters is how you feel. You wouldn't have kissed him if it didn't feel right. So, I'm happy for you."

Ki breathes a sigh of relief, then huffs out a laugh. "Good, because I really want to do it again."

Both girls giggle and then everything goes silent.

I can't stop the smile that spreads across my face as I stare down at a list of random numbers.

She wants to kiss me again. Damn, does that make me feel all kinds of warm and fuzzy inside, and definitely hard in another area too.

What was it they called it? *Amazingly earth-shattering.* It shattered my world and ruined me for anyone else.

If you'd asked me a few weeks ago, I'd have told you that one kiss could never have that effect on me, but now I know differently.

Maybe it's the years apart or the maturity, but that kiss was a million times better than the first one we had as kids.

Twenty-Seven
Makiya

I've always hated Thursdays. They're one day away from Friday, but always take way too long to be over. Of course, for me, Fridays don't mean much because we're open on Saturdays as well.

This Thursday, however, has felt extra-long because tonight is the Spring Family Night at Hannah's school.

I spend the entire day counting down the hours until I'll be out with Hunter and Hannah as a family.

I'm giddy as I dance around the café, sprucing things up in between customers.

"Someone looks like they're happy today," a familiar voice says from behind me. I turn and find London standing there, a smirk on her face.

"London!" I smile. "What are you doing here?"

"I needed a coffee break, of course! I've been so busy with Brayden and the hotel. I was so grateful that my day off fell on a school day this week. I needed some me time." London pushes back a long strand of blonde hair.

London and I had gotten close after my mom died. She had lost her own mother right after she gave birth to her son Brayden, so she knew exactly what I was going through and walked that road with me.

She's a blessing to me.

And girl's night would definitely not be the same without her!

"Well, you came to the right place." I move to give her a hug. "Have a seat, and I'll get you some food. What do you want?"

She laughs softly and says, "I'll just have some coffee and a chocolate croissant."

"Got it." I turn and get her order together.

We are due to close in a little under an hour and the lunch rush has died down, so, I grab a coffee for myself, too. I join London at the table, placing the coffee and croissant in front of her. "So, how've you been since I last saw you?"

London takes a sip of her coffee. "Same as usual. Nothing too exciting. Although, if Brent doesn't get off my back at the hotel, we might have a murder on our hands."

"Is it that bad?"

"I took the management position because I knew it would be good for us, but I didn't expect that I would spend more time at the hotel than I do with my son. Even on my days off, I'm always waiting for a call to drag me in because Brent can't hire a competent assistant or night manager. Last week, they called me at two in the morning because they couldn't find the key to the office. It was literally in the same place it always is." London delicately picks up the croissant in front of her and takes a bite. "Mm, I forgot how delicious these were."

"Yea, you definitely need to get out more," I laugh as I sip on my coffee.

London lays the croissant back down and leans back in her chair, crossing her legs and placing her hands in her lap. "I may not have any exciting news, but I hear you do." She winks at me.

And I've officially made the town gossip.

"I see that even with your busy life, you still have connections with the gossip tree."

Sabrina sticks her head out of the kitchen, waves at London, and peers at me sheepishly. "Sorry, that was my fault. London, glad you could come in today. I'd come join you, but that one," she points to me, "has me back here prepping for tomorrow."

I shrug my shoulders and take a sip of coffee, not looking at her. "Payback for telling the entire world about me and Hunter."

"You didn't even know I told London when you made me the baker for today," Sabrina glares at me, but she isn't really angry. She loves me too much. "Besides, she knew most of it already, anyway!"

"Whatever," I say, waving my hand in her direction. Sabrina laughs and disappears back into the kitchen.

"Sometimes I forget how entertaining you two can be." London shakes her head and chuckles.

"We're practically sisters. It comes with the territory," I state, trying to keep my face neutral, even though I want to laugh.

"Yea, I'm sure. Now, tell me about this news that has the whole town talking," She prods, nudging me with her foot.

I roll my eyes at her before speaking. "We kissed."

I don't need to say more than that because she knows who I'm talking about.

"No way," she gasps, her mouth hanging open and her eyes practically bulging out of their sockets.

"It's not that surprising, is it?"

"I mean you did say it wasn't like that," she smirks, reminding me of the comment I made a few weeks back at our girls' night.

"Yea, well, no one said I was smart," I joke, shrugging my shoulders.

London laughs. "I don't think being smart has anything to do with it. Horny for a hunk of delicious man? Yes. Feelings for the father of your child? Yes. Denying that you really do have feelings? Definitely. But smart? Hell no."

I roll my eyes and take a sip of my coffee. "You don't know what you're talking about."

"Yea, sure." She smiles. "All jokes aside though I'm happy for you and Hannah. Every child deserves to have their father around. Well, mine deserves to have a father, but not his biological jackass of a father."

London's boyfriend had left her when he found out she was pregnant when she was nineteen, like me. Her mom died in a car accident not too long after she had her son, so she had to do the whole thing on her own. That's one thing I admire about her: her strength.

I don't think I could have done it without my mom and dad. I'm strong, but nowhere near *that* strong. My mom had set me up for life with the café, and my dad is always there to help out with Hannah, something I'm so grateful for.

I smile. "You know what, me too, even if I've been denying it this entire time."

"Ah, denial. Thank you for finally admitting it." She giggles, stacking her dishes on the table. "Well, I should be going, but I'll see you at the fair tonight?" London asks as she stands and picks up her purse.

"I'll be there. It was great to see you. Don't be such a stranger."

She walks around the table and gives me a hug. "I can't make any promises, but I'll try not to." She waves to me as she heads towards the door.

I collect the mugs and lone plate from the table, then head to the back to start the closing routine.

London is right. I have been denying a lot of things, especially my feelings for Hunter.

If I were being honest with myself, I'd admit that my crazy heart is so in love with the one man it shouldn't be.

But denial is just so much easier. And a hell of a lot less painful.

Twenty-Eight

Hunter

I walk through the front doors of the elementary school with Hannah tugging on my arm. "Daddy, we need to move faster. We don't want to miss all the good stuff."

Ki walks beside me, her arms crossed protectively in front of her chest. She looks like the typical southern woman with her long red sundress, dark denim jacket, and cream-colored sandals. "Yea, *daddy* move faster," she giggles.

I have the sudden urge to pinch her butt in retaliation, but I decide against it. Probably not the best thing to do in an elementary school.

She knows I'll get her back for her sass later.

"Hannah, everything will still be there when we get to it," I insist as she continues to pull me through the school.

We finally stop in front of a small craft booth just inside the cafeteria. Macaroni necklaces, friendship bracelets, and other items cover the table.

Ki places her hand on my shoulder and points to a space on the table. Hannah's name is displayed beneath a set of jewelry she'd made from yarn and beads.

Hannah tugs on my arm. "Look at what I made, Daddy!" she exclaims as she locates her crafts. She lifts one of them up to me and asks, "Isn't it beautiful?"

"It's gorgeous, princess. How did you make it?" I respond, holding the beaded necklace in my hands.

"Ms. Valentine helped me, but it was easy. I just used some beads and string." I hand the necklace back to her and she puts it around her neck.

"You're so good with her," Ki whispers in my ear. She doesn't know how happy hearing that makes me.

"Hannah, I see you found your crafts." Ms. Valentine makes her way around another booth towards us. "I see both of your parents are here, too." A fake smile covers her face.

I don't miss the snark in her comment, and it kind of pisses me off.

Ki tenses beside me and forces a smile.

When Ki doesn't respond, I wrap my arm around her waist and pull her close to me. "Of course, I wouldn't miss bringing my girls to family night," I tell Ms. Valentine as politely as I can manage.

Really, I want to tell her to get over it. I told her I wasn't interested. Ki didn't have anything to do with it. I don't care what she thinks about me, but she needs to leave Ki alone.

"Very well," she mumbles. "Enjoy your evening." She waves to Hannah and walks away.

I let out a deep sigh. "I'm sorry about that."

Ki relaxes in my arms. "It's not your fault. You know, I used to like her a lot, but not so much anymore."

"Why, because you're jealous?" I goad her on with a smirk.

"No, because she didn't have the decency not to flirt with you in front of our daughter."

"But you flirt with me all the time in front of Hannah."

She smacks me on the chest and laughs. "Oh, whatever." She turns back to Hannah who is investigating the other crafts on the table. "Alright, Hannah, where to next?"

She puts her forefinger to her face and taps her lips in thought. She is too cute, and way too grown up sometimes. "Let's go play some games. There's a hard one that I think I can win." She flashes a bright smile at me.

"Bring it on," I shout excitedly.

Everyone in the cafeteria stops to look at me. "Daddy, you have to use your inside voice," Hannah says sternly, her face scrunched up and a finger pointed at me.

"Oops, sorry, I should have said that a little quieter."

"Ya think?" Ki mutters sarcastically.

I wave her off. "Like you were being quiet," I add with my own sarcasm.

"Can we go now?" Hannah asks with an exaggerated eye roll.

I laugh and grab Hannah's hand. "Alright, lead the way."

Hannah guides us outside to where more booths are set up with plenty of family friendly games. They're all created or built by the students in the elementary school which makes it all ten times as cute and awesome. As we walk by, I spot a makeshift skee ball, homemade cornhole, and even a creative milk jar toss.

This school fair was way better than any county or state fair. Although, I may be a little biased, knowing Hannah helped to make some of these games.

Hannah drags us over to a corner where a young blonde woman stands with a scrawny, brown haired boy.

Ki rushes to her and wraps her in a hug. "London, I'm so glad you made it."

I don't have any clue who she is, which isn't surprising.

As they step away from each other, London studies me. She leans into Ki and mumbles what sounds like, "He's still gorgeous."

Ki rolls her eyes, a hint of a smile gracing her lips. She motions for me to come over. "Hunter, this is my friend London. She was a few years ahead of us in school. And this is her son, Brayden."

I shake her hand and fist bump the kid. "Nice to meet you both."

"It's a pleasure to meet you. I've heard so many wonderful things about you from...Oof!" Ki elbows her in the side.

That's my girl. Always fierce.

I turn my eyes on Ki, trying to read her. A soft blush creeps to her cheeks as she looks anywhere but at me. "Is that so?"

Ki's gaze finally lands on me as she places her hands on her hips. A defensive stance I've noticed Hannah mimics a lot. "No, it's not. Until today, I hadn't even spoke to her since girls' night."

"It's true," London agrees with a sheepish look on her face. "I'm a manager at The Grand Sun Hotel. All I do is work." Brayden nods his head up and down quickly. She lays her arm around his shoulders and pulls him in. "Clearly, my son agrees."

"We were going to play some games. Would you two like to join?" Ki offers.

London waves off her offer. "No, it's okay. We don't want to intrude on your family night."

"It wouldn't be an intrusion," I insist. "In fact, we could use some extra competition."

Surprisingly, I don't really mind.

It's kind of refreshing seeing Ki with other people and meeting her friends like it's the first time again. It's something I hadn't realized I needed until now.

"See? We'd love for you to join." Ki motions between her and I.

London finally gives in with huff. "Okay, fine, so what are we playing first?"

Brayden and Hannah both point to the cornhole game at the same time. "That one!" they yell in unison as they run towards the game.

Ki is the first one behind them. "Boys against girls," she yells back to me and London.

"She seems happy," London speaks so softly I almost miss it.

"I hope she is."

"Is this what you really want?" she asks, motioning her hands around the crowded playground.

"Yea, I think so."

I mean I want to know my daughter, and I want to be with Ki, but things are still so up in the air between us.

I still have no clue where Ki really stands with us. I've made my intentions as clear as can be, but she hasn't quite voiced it to me.

As we step closer to the cornhole game, she stops and faces me with an intensity I can only attribute to her love for Ki. "*I think so* isn't good enough. She's been through a lot over the last few years, so you better *know so* soon. She's one of the best people I know. She deserves a happy ending, and if you can't give that to her, then you need to leave."

Why does everyone think I'm going to hurt Ki? And why do they keep suggesting I leave? I'm not going anywhere.

I won't lie though. London's words may piss me off, but they do make me stop and think.

Is this really what I want?

I know it is.

I think.

Twenty-Nine

Makiya

London stops Hunter on the way over to the game. Curiosity gets the best of me, and I find myself trying to read their lips, but London turns her head from me so I can't.

Dang best friend telepathy. She must have read my mind.

At least, I have a hunch on what she's telling him, though. I'd guess she's warning him not to hurt me. It's just who she is: protective. Especially of me.

I always wanted a big sister when I was younger, and that's what London has become to me.

They take the last few steps to the cornhole game and I walk over to Hunter, placing my hand on his arm to show him I care.

"Everything okay?" I ask softly, even though I already know the answer.

The look in his eyes tells me he isn't okay at all.

"Yea, everything's fine." He puts on his best fake smile and walks over to Brayden.

He uses that smile as a shield, always has, especially when he doesn't want to talk about things.

"You ever played?" he asks Brayden who stares up at Hunter with wide eyes.

Brayden is such a sweet, timid kid, especially as he looks up at the skyscraper of a man in front of him. He simply nods, too afraid to speak.

Hunter leans down to Brayden's level and gives him a high five. "Let's do this!"

Brayden's shoulders relax a little and he laughs.

I had forgotten how good Hunter is with kids.

It's one thing to see him with our daughter, but it's something else completely to see him with someone else's child. I feel the sudden need to fan myself even though it's fairly cool outside.

Damn hormones.

Nothing is more attractive than watching a man with a child, at least in my opinion. And I can't deny I find him *very* attractive at the moment.

I make my way back over to London and Hannah, the two of them, discussing strategies on how to win. "What are you doing to my daughter?"

London lifts her serious face to mine. "Turning her into a warrior with a fighting passion to win."

"I don't think you'll have much work to do. She's got the *fighting passion to win* thing down." I lift a brow and tip my head knowingly towards Hannah.

As if on cue, Hannah's hands drop immediately to her hips as she purses her lips.

That's my girl, the fighting, warrior princess. Not just her costume the year before for Halloween, courtesy of London.

"Can we get this game started?" Hunter yells back at us.

Hannah turns to him, sticks her tongue out, and lifts her arms up to show off her biceps. "Bring it on." Her face is hard, and she uses her *you don't want to mess with me* tone.

I bust out laughing as Hunter's eyes grow wider. He looks to me and lifts a brow as if to say, "you taught her that, didn't you?"

London bends over next to me snorting as she tries to hold in her laughter.

I put my hands up in front of me with my palms facing towards him. "Don't look at me. She did it!" I point my thumb at London.

She pinches me on the back of my arm and I yelp. "Ow, what was that for?"

"You know she gets the attitude from you. I just taught her how to use it effectively." She glares at me, trying to hold back the smile that threatens to form on her lips.

"Yea, yea, yea, let's just do this thing," I mutter.

Four games of cornhole, five games of skee ball, and several tosses at the milk jars later, I follow Hunter as he carries a sleeping Hannah into the house.

Dad left the door unlocked for us, knowing I probably hadn't taken a house key with me since Hunter drove today.

That's one thing I am terrible about. It drives my overly paranoid father nuts. He hates leaving the door unlocked, even though very few things ever happen in our small town.

Not to mention, we don't have anything of actual value worth stealing.

Hunter stops just outside the living room and looks at me questioningly.

"We can take her upstairs. Let me just tell my dad good night," I tell him.

I stride into the living room, kiss my dad on the cheek and whisper, "I love you."

He wraps a lone arm around me.

"He better not be here in the morning," he grumbles as I start to leave the room.

Of course, that's his response. Good ole Dad.

I glance back at my father, noting the wrinkles of fatigue around his eyes. "Daddy, I wouldn't dream of letting him stay the night."

"Good girl."

Eh, I try.

I step back out into the hallway and motion for Hunter to follow me upstairs.

Our house isn't large by any means – a simple three-bedroom, two bath house - but it was the perfect house to grow up in. It's cozy and homey, and I still feel the comfort it's always provided as I climb the fairly short staircase to the second level.

The one thing I could always count on through the good and the bad was the feeling of being *home* that hits whenever I walk into this house.

I stop in front of the first door on the left at the top of the staircase, flick the light on, and head straight to Hannah's dresser. Hunter stands in the doorway, taking up most of the space.

"What should I do?" he asks, awkwardly looking around the room.

"You can lay her down on the bed. I'm getting her pajamas real quick."

Hunter carries her over to the bed and lays her down gently as I pull out Hannah's favorite pair of unicorn pajamas.

My baby girl is the epitome of a beautiful, unique soul. She loves all things magical and charming, especially unicorns, as clearly evidenced by the number of unicorn items all over her room.

I cross over to the bed where Hunter leans awkwardly against the wall. "Are you really going to put her pj's on?" he asks as I bend over Hannah's sleeping form.

"Yes."

"Won't you wake her up?"

"Nah, she sleeps like the dead. She won't even notice," I answer, slipping her shoes and clothes off and replacing them with her pajamas.

Hunter tenses behind me as I begin changing her clothes. Once I finish, I shift her body so that her head lays on the pillow. I pull her blanket over top of her as I lean down to give her a kiss on the forehead.

When I stand back up, I notice Hunter has stepped away from us and stands back towards the door. I smile. "You can say good night."

He hesitates a second before moving back towards the bed. "I wasn't sure how you'd feel about that."

He leans down touching his lips softly to her cheek.

"You're her dad. It's your right."

He swings his head towards me, and a smile plays on his lips. "Thank you for that."

He runs his fingers over Hannah's cheek, gives her one last kiss, then stands to his full height. "She looks so precious when she's sleeping."

"Yea, she does."

He motions for me to leave the room ahead of him. I turn on her unicorn nightlight and shut off the lights, pulling the door closed behind us.

Once we're in the hallway, everything feels awkward between us. I don't know what to say or do next.

Hunter points his head toward my bedroom door. "Your room still look the same?"

"Pretty much."

"Can I see for myself?"

I move my hand toward my bedroom door. "Feel free, but I promise it isn't nearly as exciting as Hannah's. There are no unicorns to be found."

"I can live with that," he chuckles, opening the door to my room.

I stand behind him, noting just how little had really changed in my room since high school. I've never been big on change.

"You took down all the posters," Hunter comments as he points a finger to the far wall where soft shadows remain.

"Yea, I figured that as an adult I should at least have a room with no boy bands or pop singers watching my every move."

"Makes sense."

Hunter sits down on my bed and pats the spot next to him. I join him, loving the way it feels to be with him like this again, but also worrying about all the ways it can go wrong.

He wraps his arm around my shoulder and pulls me in close. "We used to spend so much time in here growing up." He tilts my head up so I am looking at him. "You know, I wish I could go back and do things over."

I do know. And I know it's hard for him to see the results from his decisions. I can see the regret in his eyes that's eating him alive.

"It's not how I wanted things to go obviously, but it made me the woman I am now. My mom always told me things happen for a reason, and I know she was right." I lay my head back on his shoulder still gazing up at him. "One thing I've learned is that love is crazy, Hunter. Those feelings make us do crazy things, and sometimes become crazy people, but I have to believe that love is worth all the crazy that comes with it. I mean we wouldn't have Hannah, I probably wouldn't be running the café, and I probably wouldn't have the relationship I have with my father."

"Crazy love, I like that," Hunter whispers as his lips move closer to mine.

Our lips collide in one sweeping movement. Passion overtakes us. He forces my lips open with his, taking in all of me.

He tastes of mint and chocolate, his two favorite things, and I revel in the feel of his lips on mine again.

His other arm wraps around me as he pulls me onto his lap, deepening the kiss. I want so much more than this. The need grows stronger inside me as I grasp his shirt, trying to get closer to him.

This is such a bad idea, but one I can't quite let go of just yet.

Thirty

Hunter

I stand next to my brother on the beachfront outside the one and only fancy hotel in Sunrise. An arch of beautiful tiger lilies stands directly behind us in the only remaining grassy part before reaching the sand. The ocean roars a few yards away, giving us a beautiful background of blue rolling waves.

The wedding planner is off to the side, directing the wedding party to their places and explaining the plan for the ceremony and reception.

I, of course, am the best man. I mean, who else would my brother pick? Even if I haven't been home in five years, we've stayed close. Besides, it's not like we have any real friends outside each other. At least, not ones that are males.

I study my brother's face as Meg makes her way down the aisle towards us. Granted it's only the rehearsal, but he looks so happy when he sees her, a goofy smile spreads across his face that says it all.

I resist the urge to roll my eyes. It isn't even the wedding, but you would never know that from the huge grin on his face.

Just like you can't tell that I had the best make out session of my life last night by the grin on *my* face.

Physically, I wanted to turn that kiss into so much more, but mentally, I couldn't allow myself to do it.

Mostly because her dad knocked on the door just as things were getting good.

Meg stops in front of Riley, and the wedding planner stops them to discuss the rest of the ceremony. When she's finished, we're released to the bar for drinks and dinner.

I clap a hand on my brother's back as I walk with him to the hotel. "You nervous yet?" I ask.

"Hell, no, I'm excited. Tomorrow, I'm going to be the luckiest man on Earth."

"Isn't the groom supposed to be nervous the day before his wedding?" I ask as we continue to follow the path.

"Not when you know you're marrying the right woman." Riley looks back at me, happiness in his eyes.

"How did you know she was the right one?" I ask, genuinely curious because I have no clue what I'm doing when it comes to women.

Example One: Makiya

I had run out on the only woman who'd ever meant anything to me. So how do you know when you've finally found the right one?

He pauses in the middle of the path. "Promise me you won't make fun of me if I tell you this?" His face is stern, his eyes hard.

I try not to laugh as people pass around us, but it's hard. Like me last night with Ki.

"Is it going to be completely cheesy? Because if it is, I can't make any promises."

"Probably, yea," he laughs and starts walking again. "I knew because she was the one girl I couldn't get out of my head. The minute I saw her, I was done. She was it for me, even though I tried to fight it from the beginning. I kept coming back to her, and that's how I knew."

Yea, that's cheesy as hell, but it also makes complete sense to me.

Because I know exactly what he means.

Even after all this time, I'm still drawn to Ki. I tried desperately in college to get her out of my head by sleeping with any and every girl, but it hadn't worked.

Is that because she's the one for me? Is it because I'd always been in love with her?

Probably. I mean, that was the whole reason I ran. Loving her scared the shit out of me. *Then.* But now…not so much.

Riley stops to open the back door of the hotel. "Let's get a drink."

When we reach the bar, he orders both of us a local craft beer. We stand there joking around and catching up while we wait for dinner to start.

Riley points at me with his beer. "So, how're things going with Ki?"

"Good, I think." I take a sip of my beer because I'm at a loss for what else to say.

I haven't really talked to anyone about me and Ki, and I don't really count the conversation with London since I didn't do any talking.

I'm so afraid that I'll screw things up between us again if I talk about it. It's superstitious and ridiculous, and I know that. But I can't help myself, I want things to work.

"You think?" Riley asks as he waves the bartender down for another beer.

"Yea, I think you're going to be wasted before dinner if you don't stop drinking so damn fast."

Riley shakes his head as he takes a large gulp from his fresh beer. "Don't change the subject. Besides, I'm getting married tomorrow. I'm supposed to get drunk tonight."

My brother is ridiculous. "I think you're supposed to get drunk after your wedding not before."

"Oh, what do you know? You've never been married." He waves me off as he takes an even bigger gulp.

"No, but I've been to my fair share of weddings. Getting drunk the night before never leads to anything good."

"Fine, I'll slow down." Riley places his beer on the bar and looks at me. "I'll ask again. How're things with Ki?"

I sit my empty bottle on the bar in front of me. "From my side, things are going great, but I'm still not entirely sure how Ki feels."

"Well, have you asked her?" Riley prods.

"No," I say.

"Why not?"

"The other night, we ran into her friend London at the family fair, and she gave me some tough love about Ki."

"Ah, London. She's the best that way - honest, blunt, always to the point. Look, she's just trying to protect Ki. The same as Sabrina and everyone else."

I play with the label on the bottle in front of me, knowing my brother is right, but London's words have made me question everything I thought I knew about my feelings for Ki.

The bartender walks passed and motions towards my beer. "You want another?"

I shake my hand. "No, thanks, I'm good." He gives me a thumbs up and walks away.

Riley pats me on the back. "Hunter, just talk to her about it. I'm sure she's feeling the same way you are about everything, but you have to be a man and ask her. As for London, she's not the one who has the final decision. Ki does. Figure out what you really want, then talk to Ki."

"I don't want to lose her again, and I think it's way too soon to put any pressure on us. I just got her to agree to let me spend time with her and Hannah. I don't want to ruin it."

"Sounds to me like you're just making excuses. At some point, you're going to have to stop hiding and face your feelings."

"I'm not hiding from my feelings." I say, slightly offended by my brother's statement. I don't want to ruin things, but I'm not scared of how I feel. Right?

I practically announced to the whole town that we're a thing. Surely, that doesn't constitute as hiding your feelings.

"You sure about that?" Riley lifts his left brow, prodding me to argue with him. "If you ask me, you two were always meant to be together, but you never wanted to admit it." He points towards the door that leads to the banquet hall, promptly ending the conversation. "Let's go before Meg comes looking for us."

We walk to the dinner in silence, leaving me to process all the shit that just came out of my brother's mouth alone.

Saturday morning comes faster than I expect. I roll over, shut off my alarm and get ready. I'm supposed to meet Ki at the cafe to watch Hannah for the day, even though I should technically be with my brother all day. Thank goodness, Riley understood when I told him I was going to spend the day with my daughter.

When Ki's done working, we're all going to the wedding together.

I slide into my jeans and an ice blue button up and slip my favorite pair of Nikes on my feet. I take a quick peek in the mirror and adjust my shirt.

Ki will definitely approve.

I head downstairs to the kitchen and pour myself a small cup of coffee into a travel mug, knowing I can refill it at the café.

Perks of dating a woman who can bake and make great coffee.

Fifteen minutes later, I pull into the back lot of the café just as Ki and Hannah are pulling in. I climb out and brace myself to catch Hannah as she shoots out of the car and into my arms. "Hey, there, princess."

"Mommy said I get to spend the day with you, then we get to see Uncle Riley and Aunt Meg get married."

I can't help the way those words still get to me. The fact she knew them but didn't know me. Not to mention, I'm curious if she ever asked them about me. Was she ever curious how they were related to her?

I suppose it's possible she assumed they were Ki's family since Ki seems to be so close to them. I guess that's something I should ask them one day.

"That's right," I say, squeezing her tight. I move her into my left arm so I can greet Ki with a sideways hug. "I thought you'd have been here by now."

She leans into my side, "Since I was bringing Hannah this morning, I asked Sabrina to open for me. This munchkin takes forever to get out of bed." She tickles Hannah's side and Hannah giggles.

I love seeing my girl happy.

Yep, I'm a sap.

"Stop, Mommy, that tickles." Hannah squirms in my arms trying to get away from Ki.

She pulls her hands back. "Okay, I have to get in there and get ready to open since Aunt Sabrina is never on time. I love you, kid." She kisses Hannah on the cheek. She looks to me and shoves an accusing finger in my face, "Don't have too much fun today. I think I still deserve to be the favorite parent."

I push her finger away and chuckle. "Can't make any promises."

That seems to be my motto, one I'm definitely going to need to change.

She throws her head back and laughs. "Okay, I really need to get in there. I'll see you this evening. 4:00, right?"

I nod. "I'll bring Hannah with me. Mom will help her get ready, then we'll run by and grab you."

"Perfect," she agrees as she heads towards the café. *I can definitely get used to that,* I think as my eyes land on the gentle sway of her hips as she dips inside the café.

Maybe Riley's right, maybe I'd always known, but just never wanted to admit it. And maybe a part of me is still a little too scared to admit it.

I want all of it with Ki.

Thirty-One
Makiya

I glance at myself in the mirror one last time. My smokey eyeshadow enhances my brown eyes, making them look like chocolate. The purple V-neck dress I wear hugs my curves in just the right places, just like I'd intended.

I want to see that look of hunger in Hunter's eyes when he sees me like he'd given me the night we kissed. I've tried to rationalize my feelings toward him, but I can't.

It doesn't make sense to me that after all the time that has passed, I still feel the same about him. I guess love is crazy like that.

I had always known Hunter was my one person. It's why I never pursued anyone after he left. Well, that and fear.

But as the years passed, I felt the feelings towards him fading away, almost like I was over him. Only, I knew they had never really left me.

Spending so much time with Hunter again has proven that to me, but just because my heart feels this way about him doesn't mean my head does.

In fact, my head criticizes me every day for getting too close to him. My mind constantly reminds me of all the ways he's hurt me before, but it isn't that easy to make your heart listen to your head.

From outside comes a honk from what I assume is Hunter's truck. I try to reason with myself again that this is good for Hannah and me, even if it ends in heartbreak again.

My heart needs to find out if what I feel for him is true, or if it is just the crazy attraction that has buzzed between us since puberty.

I slap a layer of lip gloss on, look at myself one last time, and grab my purse before flying down the stairs. I yell a quick good-bye to my dad as I step outside onto the front porch.

Hannah waves at me from the backseat of Hunter's truck. Her hair is in a crown braid and the pieces left down are curled.

Hunter jumps out of the truck and walks around the front as I move towards him. His eyes slowly make their way from my feet to my head, stopping momentarily on the tops of my breasts where the neckline hits.

He whistles and motions for me to turn around with his finger. "Damn, Ki, you look amazing."

I roll my eyes at him because he knows I despise the catcall, but I turn around anyway. As I turn back to face him, I curtsy because what the hell, I'm feeling sassy as usual.

"Thank you. You don't look too shabby yourself." I nod my approval as I study the way the tuxedo clings to the bulging muscles in his arms.

He puts his right hand out to the side, palm side up. "Your carriage awaits," he says as he bows deeply, barely keeping a straight face.

Instantly, I'm suspicious. He doesn't do prince charming romantics.

"Stand up, Hunter, I know you. You've never been a gentleman around me." I eye him curiously. He's up to something.

"People change." He shrugs his shoulders as he straightens out the wrinkles now visible on his tux.

"Maybe, but I bet you have something else up your sleeve."

The corner of his lip lifts slightly as his eyes tease me. "Guess you'll find out, won't you?"

I reach for his hand and pull the bottom of my dress up slightly as I climb into his truck. He's definitely hiding something, and he knows I hate surprises which means his lips are also sealed until it's time.

Sometimes, I really despise how well he knows me.

A few minutes later, we pull into the parking lot of the Grand Sun Hotel.

Sunrise has a thing for keeping the name of the town in every business within its limits. I don't know for sure if it's a requirement but considering every business on Main Street has "sun" or "rise" in their name, I assume it is.

I look up at the beautiful beach-front hotel laid out in front of me. It's at least five stories high and the length of a football field, maybe more.

I'm not really good at the whole math thing.

The hotel has been in Sunrise for over fifty years and has garnered the respect of several celebrities and wealthy families over the years. It's a little expensive and uppity for my taste, but I can't deny what a beautiful place it is for a wedding.

I jump down from Hunter's truck like a practiced pro.

Well, more like I stumble out of Hunter's big ass truck.

I hear his laughter from beside me. "You forget how to get out of a truck?"

"I mean you could be more considerate and not have it lifted up so high. After all, I'm pretty short." I stick my tongue out at him.

"I could, *but* then it wouldn't be nearly as much fun watching you get out of the truck." His lopsided grin leaves me feeling a little weak in the knees.

Why does he have to be so damn good-looking?

I know this night is bound to be trouble for me. But it'll be the good kind of trouble.

Hannah jumps out of the truck much more gracefully than me thanks to the help of Hunter. She grins up at me just like her dad. "See? It's not that hard."

I wiggle my fingers in front of her face. "I'm sorry. What did you say? I think I heard you say, 'Mommy, tickle me, please.'"

She immediately runs to hide behind Hunter's legs. "I didn't say anything," she screeches, laughing.

"That's what I thought." I tap my finger on my chin and she giggles some more.

I love hearing her laugh. I love seeing her so unbelievably happy, and it's even better because I'm happy too.

"Well, you girls look beautiful!" Riley says as he strides over to us from the entrance of the hotel.

"Hey, brother, how're you feeling today?" Hunter reaches to shake his hand and pulls him in for a hug.

"I won't lie. I'm a little nervous, but mostly excited for this whole thing to be done with so we can celebrate. I needed to get some fresh air though," he admits, reaching in to give me and Hannah a hug.

"I'm super happy for you, Riley. You and Meg are so great together," I gush as he steps back.

The smile on his face can't be contained. It's so big and so bright that I kind of want to smile with him.

"Come on, let's go inside." He waves his hand for us to follow him in.

He and Hunter make small talk about the wedding and the guests already there as we walk inside the hotel and out the back door. Lilies of all colors line the pathway down to the beach. I love lilies almost as much as Meg does.

We follow the path until we reach the numerous lines of white chairs in front of the most beautiful and intricately decorated arch I've ever seen.

A lone tear slides down my face as the beauty of the area catches my breath. I always thought this would be me and Hunter someday.

He steps away from Riley and reaches over to wipe the tear off my cheek. "I know what you're thinking, and this *will* be us one day," he whispers in my ear.

I want to believe him so much, but I just don't know how.

I gaze into his light eyes and see a multitude of emotions swirling around in them. He has to be feeling the same way I am. It's the only way to explain the sadness and regret that lingers in his eyes.

I can't get my hopes up. I'll just enjoy my time with him (especially the sizzling, hot kisses), but I won't let myself think it can be more.

Thirty-Two

Hunter

Everything about the wedding makes me wonder what mine and Ki's will look like some day.

I'd told Ki it would be us, and I had meant it.

I'm still having trouble processing where we are as a couple, but that has more to do with not knowing where Ki stands rather than me not knowing. I need to know how Ki feels if we're going to make this thing work.

I know she loves me in a sense - she told me as much growing up. But had that turned into romantic love? And if it had, does she still feel that way now?

My mom, Riley, and even London seem to think she does, but how can I be sure?

What if her fear of me leaving is stronger than her love for me? I know how powerful fear can be, it's what ran me off.

It doesn't matter right now, though. What matters is spending time with my girls and celebrating my brother's wedding.

Besides, I have a surprise set up for me and Ki after the reception that will give us some much-needed time alone to talk and do other things.

Dirty things.

At least, I hope those things will happen.

I sit at my designated Table #2 and watch as Ki and Hannah dance, scrunched between the other hundred bodies or so on the dance floor. They both had begged me to join, but I'm not a big dancer.

When a slow song comes on, Ki looks over at me wistfully and grabs onto Hannah to dance with her.

The fifth time it happens I feel a nudge against my shoulder. "You should go dance with her. Clearly, she wants you to," Riley urges, pushing me a little harder this time.

"I don't dance," I grumble, crossing my arms in front of me.

"Make an exception for your girl. Trust me, she'll love it more than any damn gift you could think of to give her."

Slowly, I stand.

Not because I want too, but because I know Riley won't leave it alone.

I move slowly toward the dance floor, hoping the song will be over by the time I reach it.

Unfortunately, Riley doesn't give me the option to take my time. Instead, he shoves me so hard onto the dance floor that I nearly knock Ki to the ground.

She turns to me and covers her mouth to hide her giggle. "What are you doing?"

"Riley," I mutter. I reach my hand out to her, but she doesn't move to take it.

Come on, girl. Don't make me beg.

Beg. Begging actually sounds really good right now, but not coming from me. Coming from *her* as I …

Nope. I can't think like this right now. I'm in the middle of the dance floor with my daughter a few feet away, dancing with my dad.

Ki tilts her head to the side. "I know you don't like dancing. You don't have to be out here."

I push my hand closer to her. "I know but I want to be."

She lifts a brow, knowing I'm lying, but she grabs my hand anyway. I place my hands on her hips and she wraps hers around my neck.

I thought I hated dancing, but I like this slow dancing shit. I pull Ki closer to me and she leans her head on my chest.

It feels right.

To be here, with her in my arms.

I enjoy the moment, allowing my eyes to follow Hannah and my dad around the dance floor as I hold Ki close. I'm not about to let Hannah out of my sight, even if we are surrounded by family.

When the song ends, Ki steps back from me and smiles. "Wanna grab another drink?"

"Hell yea, I do." I follow her to the bar where we both order our drinks.

Once she has her wine and I have my whiskey, I pull her off to the side of the bar into a little alcove.

"What are you doing?" she questions, swallowing a sip of white wine.

"I have a surprise for you." I pull a key card to a hotel room out of my pocket.

I feel like a damn teenager holding it in my hand, but what else am I supposed to do when we both live with our parents and Hannah?

"Mom offered to watch Hannah tonight so you and I could spend some time alone. I rented us a hotel room here so that we don't have to drive anywhere." I try to give her the keycard in my hand, but she refuses to take it.

"Hunter," she sighs. "I can't."

I put my hand in the air to shush her. Her eyes burn with rage.

She's about to tell me to fuck off, I can see it in her eyes, so I rush to speak, "Just hear me out, okay? I didn't get the room for us so we could have sex, even though I wouldn't mind it if it happened," I pause and she smirks at me, a hint of amusement in her eyes. "I got it because you and I haven't really spent any time alone or had a chance to talk about what we want to happen between us. And it's something I think we need to do."

"I feel like we're in high school again, and I'm about to tell you I can't stay with you because my dad and mom will be pissed. But, Hunter, come on, do you really think it's a good idea?"

Emotions swirl in her deep brown eyes. I know she's scared and maybe a little confused. It's a bold move, but one that I feel I need to make to show her how I really feel about her.

"Why would it not be?"

"After that last kiss, do you really think we'll actually be talking?" she asks smugly.

The smoldering heat coming from her eyes makes me just about die.

"Would that be such a bad thing?" Because *I* don't think so.

Hell, I'd take her up to the room right now if she'd agree.

"Yes, *ugh*, no. I don't know." Her face contorts with confusion.

"Give me your hand." She reaches her hand out to me, palm up. I place the keycard in her hand. "We won't do anything you don't want to do. I promise. Just think about it, okay? Now, shall we go dance some more?"

She places the keycard in her small purse and grasps onto the hand I hold out for her. "You hate dancing."

"But I like you, and you like dancing."

"That I do." She quirks her head at me and winks. "You keep this up and you might just get what you want."

Challenge accepted.

There is no way there will be any talking going on in that room. Definitely not if she keeps looking at me the way she is now.

Thirty-Three
Makiya

I am becoming really good at making terrible decisions. Like how I'm currently standing in an elevator, with Hunter, on the way to a hotel room where I'm pretty sure no talking will actually happen. Every part of me says this is a bad idea, that I'm repeating history, but I want him, all of him.

Preferably with no clothes on.

After our talk, he had spent the rest of the night twirling Hannah and I around the dance floor, something I hadn't expected from him considering he hates dancing. I was caught up in the moment when Rose came up to the table and told us she was taking

Hannah with her and for us to have fun. And I *was* having fun, so much that I didn't want the night to end.

And that's how I ended up in an elevator with Hunter.

He's so charming when he wants to be, and I have a weak spot in my heart for him - I always have - so it wasn't too difficult to say yes when he asked for the thousandth time if I wanted to join him in the hotel room for the night. Plus, I'm curious to know if he meant what he'd said earlier, that he really just wants to talk.

It isn't like the Hunter I know to sit and talk with a girl, especially not in a hotel room, but the Hunter that stands next to me now isn't the same one I knew in high school. He's grown up along the way.

The old Hunter isn't someone I want in my life, at least not at this point.

When I was eighteen and pregnant, I wanted nothing more than the old Hunter to be there for me, but I also knew that, at the time, it wasn't something he was capable of doing. He didn't understand what it meant to give up something you love for someone you love *more*. That was something I had needed from him then and still need from him now.

He has to be able to show me more than how attracted he is to me, which was something he'd never done when we were younger. I need him to show me he cares with more than just words and kisses because in life, those things aren't always enough to make a relationship work.

He has always known me better than anyone. But he's never had a knack for sticking through the hard things; instead, he runs from them.

What I need from him is to be an adult and prove to me he isn't going anywhere.

And, so far, the Hunter standing next to me has done that. But can he keep it up?

The elevator dings as we reach the fifth floor. It moves surprisingly slow considering there aren't that many levels, but it's also an older elevator that creaks as it moves and makes you wonder if it can actually carry you to your floor.

Hunter grabs my hand and pulls me behind him out of the elevator. I follow him to the right, then the left, where we find our room at the end of the hall.

I had lived in Sunrise my whole life, but I'd never been inside the hotel. Probably because my family is far from rich, but mostly because there was never any need to stay here.

Many of my friends in high school worked at the hotel in the summer, but I'd always had a job at my mom's café. In fact, many of them still work at the hotel now, like London. It's one of the larger employers in town, along with Hunter's dad's construction company.

Hunter unlocks the door to our room and motions for me to enter, holding the door open for me. *How chivalrous of him!* Maybe he *has* changed, or at least grown up. Old Hunter probably wouldn't have ever thought of holding the door open for me.

My jaw drops open without me even realizing it. The room is huge with a king size bed directly in the middle, a sofa in front of the window, and a 50" flat screen TV on the wall above the dresser, with multiple shades of white, gray, and black.

"You still think staying here is a bad idea?" Hunter asks next to me, reading the emotions on my face.

I shake my head. "Hell no, this room is incredible."

"Yea, it is. Brent let us tour the honeymoon suite last week so Meg and Riley could see what it looked like. While we were here, I asked about getting another suite for the two of us."

I tilt my head to the right as I look at him. "You know the owner?"

"Well, yea, Dad helped renovate some of the rooms a few years back. Part of the deal was discounted rooms as well."

"Ahh," I say. Now, I understand why we're staying here.

"You think I'm cheap now, don't you?" he laughs, shaking his head as he walks over to the bed. I remain in the hallway. I'm not done enjoying this room yet; I haven't even looked at the bathroom.

"No, I don't. I think you're very smart actually. I love a good deal," I laugh as I take a step inside the bathroom. "Oh my goodness, you need to see this bathroom!" The bathtub is humongous - like outdoor jacuzzi humongous. You can fit at least five people in it at once, and the shower is just as big.

I'm officially in love with this hotel.

Hunter sneaks up behind me and grabs me around the waist. "You know what this bathroom is perfect for?" he whispers in my ear.

I shiver with delight as a multitude of dirty images race through my mind.

No, I shake the thoughts from my head. *We are here for talking, not sexy time.*

Even though, I really, really want sexy time with him.

I shift in his arms and smack him on the shoulder. "I thought we were just talking tonight," I remind him.

He clasps his hands at my lower back, forcing me to face him. "Honey, we can do whatever the hell you want to tonight. Your wish is my command."

I chew on my bottom lip. "Hm, anything I want?" I ask shyly, hiding my eyes from him for added effect.

He pulls me closer, and I feel the hard-on springing to life inside his dress pants. "Absolutely anything."

"Well, in that case," I stand on my tiptoes, and latch my lips onto his.

Within seconds, the kiss turns into fiery passion. He pushes me up against the bathroom sink and his tongue pushes my lips apart, deepening the kiss. I'm dizzy with need, a need that's not going to go away unless I do every dirty thing that I've been dreaming about these last two weeks.

And that's exactly what I'm going to do.

Screw talking, we can do that later.

I need him *now*.

Oh shit!

What the hell did I do last night?

My head is pounding, my body snuggled up against something warm and strong.

Hunter?

No, no, no, please tell me I didn't do what I think I did.

I lift the sheet up gently, trying not to wake the snoring beast next to me.

I see nothing but skin. My naked, pale skin. I did it. I definitely did it, that dirty thing that I said I wasn't going to do with Hunter.

Why? *Why* did I do it?

What the hell is wrong with me? I'm a glutton for punishment, that's what.

Hunter clouds my judgement, makes me forget all reason. I'm a strong, sassy woman. I'm not supposed to do stupid things like forget all reason.

But, oh, did I love what happened last night when I did. Hunter took me to new places with new feelings. Feelings that emphasized my love for him.

He knows now how I really feel. There's no way he couldn't. If my eyes hadn't told him last night, my mouth definitely did.

My dumb, impulsive mouth. I was feeling all the feels, and the words. They just fell out like water pouring from a waterfall. I couldn't have stopped them even if I'd wanted too.

Last night had definitely been a bad idea, but boy do I love bad ideas.

I want to snuggle up to Hunter's warmth no matter how stupid I feel, but my fear of what Hunter will say when he wakes up is too strong. I slowly climb out of bed, trying my best not to jostle him.

At least, after this, I'll know if he really does want me, right?

I mean the way he worked on my body last night tells me he wants me, but last time we did this he left.

He said he wanted me, we had sex, and then he was gone the next day.

How can I not think that's how it will happen again? How can I not believe that it isn't me that's the problem? There were only two factors the first time, and considering he's the one that left, I'm thinking I'm the reason.

I mean, I have to be - it's the only thing that makes sense, which means I need to leave before he has the chance to leave me.

I search the room for my clothes, finding them in several places. *Man, we really went at it, didn't we?* I slip into my dress from last night and pick up my underwear to stash it in my bag.

There's no way I'm wearing gross day-old panties. I'd rather take the risk of going commando, which is exactly what I do.

Just as I'm about to open the door, there's rustling from the bed.

Go back to sleep. Please, go back to sleep.

"Hey, where are you heading off to so fast? And why didn't you wake me?"

Dang it, I've been caught. I turn slowly back around and look at Hunter. His hair sticks up all over, and his eyes look like they're still not quite functioning. He brushes his hand through his hair and yawns.

Well, guess, I don't have a choice. I walk back over to the bed and sit down awkwardly. "Was going to go find some coffee?"

He cocks an eyebrow at me. Yea, didn't think I'd get away with that one, but a girl has to try, right? "I'm not stupid. I've been in this position before. You were leaving, why?"

He lifts himself up onto his arm so he can look me in the eyes better. I can't lie again - he'll be able to tell.

"I just," I stop speaking. I don't know what to say. Everything I want to say is a lie, and I sure as hell don't want to tell him the truth.

"Ki," he says smoothly, reaching his free arm out to my thigh. He lays his hand on top of it and rubs calming circles across my skin.

Unfortunately, they aren't calming me down at all. The only thing they're accomplishing is driving my hormones crazy with lust.

I scoot away from his hand so I can think better. He's going to know I'm lying no matter what I say. he knows me too well. I don't think I have much of a choice but to be honest.

What can it hurt, right?

"The last time we did this," I mutter, motioning my hands around the room, "you left the next day."

He closes his eyes and squeezes them tight, wrinkling his nose in the process. He blows out a huff. "Shit, I did, didn't I?"

"Yea, you did," I say simultaneously nodding my head. "You dropped me off at my house. Then, you left without a word. I didn't want you to have the chance to do that again."

"Well, I mean, you were already awake, so I wouldn't have been able to leave without a word." He winks at me.

I crinkle my nose in disgust and shove him a little harder than necessary on the shoulder. "Not funny."

"Sorry," he mumbles, rubbing his shoulder where my fist just landed. "I wasn't planning on leaving without you today. You did come with me to the hotel."

"Again, not funny," I huff out through flaring nostrils. I'm pissed that he isn't taking this seriously. It's like he thinks it's some big joke, but this is my heart we're talking about. Not a damn joke.

I start to stand, but he stops me with his hand. "Look, I'm sorry. That was insensitive."

"Ya think, dumbass?"

He curls his lip up a bit into a smirk. "I guess I deserved that."

"If you don't stop acting like this is a joke, I'm going to call my dad to come pick me up. And there will be no shame as I walk to his truck in the same damn dress I left in last night."

That's a lie. There will definitely be shame.

He leans back in a defensive stance, his forearm still sitting comfortably on the bed. "Okay, okay. Let's talk, Ki."

"About what?"

"Us."

Us? There's still an "us" after last night?

Thirty-Four

Hunter

Ki looks at me as if I've said something completely crazy. Her mouth hangs open and her eyes look like they might pop out of her head at any minute.

I can't figure out why she's shocked. All I said was I want to talk about us. How could she really think there isn't an us, especially after last night?

I've had some pretty damn amazing sex in my life, but it was never as good as it was with Ki. It was like sparks exploded between us. There was no thinking, only feeling.

Especially when she said she loved me. That was the icing on the cake. I was so in the zone though that I didn't respond.

Shit. I hadn't responded. Maybe that's why she was acting the way she was today. I hadn't said those three simple words back.

Three simple words that need to be reciprocated or the other might think you don't feel the same way.

But I can't say them to her. Not yet.

She won't believe them even if I do.

Damn. Yea, we definitely need to talk about us.

I wiggle my fingers in front of her face, trying to catch her attention. "Earth to Ki. You still with me?"

She shakes her head erratically. "Yea, I'm still here. Sorry, I just really thought that after last night…" She doesn't finish her statement.

There's fear in her eyes, even more visible by the hint of tears encircling her large brown eyes. I hate that her fiery sass has disappeared, and fear is left in its wake.

Clearly, I need to step up my game.

"Ki, last night was amazing." I pause. I'm not sure exactly what to say at this point.

"But?" she questions.

"There is no but. Being with you is what made it so special, Ki. You make every day so amazing for me." I reach for the hand holding her up on the bed. She resituates herself and puts her hand in mine.

"I like that," she grins down at me.

"Yea, me too, and I want to keep having nights like that."

She chews on the inside of her cheek as she thinks about what I said. "So, you want to keep having sex with me is what you're saying?"

I chuckle. "You and that dirty mind of yours."

"You're the one who said you want to keep having nights like that, and sex is all we did last night."

"Yes, I really, really like what we did last night, but I meant I want to spend more time with you alone. Like dating, Ki. Real dating, where I take you out without Hannah and we eat some delicious food."

Her eyes crinkle in the corners as she contemplates my words. "You really mean that?"

"Yes, I do."

"You're not just saying it because we had sex?"

This whole second guessing my motives thing she keeps doing is really starting to frustrate the hell out of me. I force the feeling back, though, because I know I hurt her in the past. I need to give her time to accept that what I've been saying is true and not just some ploy to play with her emotions.

I squeeze her hand tight between my fingers. "No, I'm not just saying it because I had the best sex of my life last night. I'm saying it because I mean it. Ki, what do you say? You want to jump all in with me?"

Her lips curve up into a smile as she leans closer to me. "I do. I want to jump all in with you, but I swear if you walk out that door again, that's it. No more second chances or new beginnings."

"Technically, it would be a third chance," I point out.

She slaps me playfully on the arm. "Oh, shut up."

I pull her down the last few feet until she's laying on top of me. Her face is mere inches away from mine. She slips her hands up under my shoulders as I clasp my arms around her back.

I lift my head up, bringing my lips to hers. The kiss is chaste at first, but it quickly grows, expressing the extent of the passion I feel for her.

Our tongues clash together in a war of emotions that neither of us seem to be ready to speak, but we sure can show it.

I pull back, slowly, not really wanting too but knowing we need to finish this conversation. "Damn, that never gets old." I whisper.

She giggles in agreement.

My heart could burst with happiness right now. For the first time, I'm not terrified of making a commitment. I'm actually excited about *really* dating the one girl whose never truly left my mind or my heart. I've just been too afraid to admit that all these years.

She lays her head down on my chest and I kiss her forehead. I feel at home with her in my arms. There's no place I'd rather be than with Ki. Here. Right now. All I hope is that I can make her see that, too.

I mull over the best way to do that when an idea comes to me. "I want to take you on a date soon."

I'm desperately hoping that this is the one move I need to make to show her I'm serious about us.

"Okay," she responds wistfully.

"How about Friday night? You, me, dinner?"

"Mhm," she mumbles against my chest.

"I'll take that as a yes." My chest rumbles as I chuckle.

Ki lifts her head up and gives me a small peck on the lips. Instantly, I want more, but I know I need to take her home, so I hold off the yearning. She stares straight into my eyes. "That is definitely a yes. Just one thing, what about Hannah?"

"I'll ask Mom to watch her. I'm sure she won't mind."

"Then, it's a date."

I fist pump the air above me. I don't care how ridiculous I look or sound or even feel.

Its foreign to me to feel like this. I haven't felt this happy since that night with Ki in the back of my truck. My heart was so full that night, but it was also terrifying to think I could end up like my parents. There was nothing more horrifying than that.

Now, though, I know there's nothing scary about my parents' life. They're happy. They're healthy. And that's all I want. I think it's all I've ever really wanted. I was just too scared to admit it.

Once Ki and I are dressed and ready, I drive her back to her house where an hour before, my mom had dropped Hannah off. I give her a long kiss good-bye before heading back to my mom's house.

As I step through the door, my mom hollers from the kitchen, "Hunter, is that you?"

"Yea, it's me, Ma." I walk down the hallway to the kitchen.

Mom's holding a cup of coffee out to me, and I happily grab it from her and take a sip. She eyes me the entire time. I know she wants to know about last night, but those aren't really details that I want to talk to her about.

I sit the cup down on the counter and lean my elbows on it, looking up to my mom. "Can you watch Hannah on Friday night?"

She crosses her arms in front of her chest and stares me down. "I take it last night went well," she says in the most serious tone.

I can't tell if she's genuinely angry with me for not telling her anything or not.

"Yes," I say the word so long that the "s" comes out in a hiss.

"Okay, I want details." She still hasn't moved, and her stare has turned into more of a glare.

I flop my head down into my hands with a soft groan. My mom can't be serious. I'm a grown man, and grown men do things their mom should never know about, especially the things that happened last night.

"Hunter," she says her tone growing higher with each syllable.

"Mom, I'm not giving you details. That goes against every mother-son code out there."

She rolls her eyes, then centers them on me again. "I don't want those details, you idiot. I want the details about the conversation. Weren't you and Ki supposed to be talking last night?" She quirks her right eyebrow at me, and instantly, I feel like I'm in trouble.

"You can't call me an idiot, Mom. I'm your son."

Even though I completely forgot I'd told her I was getting a room at the hotel so we could drink and talk.

"It doesn't say I can't call you that in my handbook."

"You think I can borrow it?" I ask, jokingly.

Although a part of me is slightly serious. If only there were such a thing as a parenting handbook, 'cause I sure as shit don't know anything about it.

My mom's face falls. "You know you're a great dad, Hunter. Hannah clearly loves you already. You don't need a handbook to tell you what to do."

I hear her, but I don't believe her. "Sometimes, I feel like I've got it. Then, other days, I feel like I have no idea what I'm doing."

My mom pushes off from the counter and takes a step closer to me. "That's how all parents feel, but you also are just getting to know Hannah. It comes with time. Give yourself that time. Now, back to last night. How did the talk go with Ki?"

"Do you think I would have asked you to watch Hannah on Friday if it hadn't gone well?"

Mom's face lights up with laughter. "I suppose not. Of course I'll watch Hannah on Friday."

"Good, because I'm taking Ki on our first date."

My mom grabs both my shoulders and pulls me in for a hug. "You don't know how happy that makes me."

But she's wrong. I know exactly how happy that makes her because it makes me just as happy.

A committed, family man. Who would have ever thought I'd be happy about that?

Thirty-Five
Makiya

The week slipped by quickly, as it always seems to do when I'm looking forward to something. When Friday rolls around, Hunter and I had found an even better rhythm than before once we clarified exactly where we stood.

On Monday, he showed up at the house before I left to watch Hannah and take her to school. At first, Dad grumbled about that because it was his special time, but I reminded him he was the one who said Hunter deserved a chance. Dad couldn't argue with me about that.

So, Hunter started doing the morning drops offs and we both picked Hannah up from school. Then, we would have dinner at my house or at his place, depending on who was home. After dinner, we worked together to get Hannah ready for bed.

I can't even begin to explain how wonderful it has been to have Hunter here to share all these things with me now.

I've never really liked having help from someone else; I'm more the type to do everything on my own. I've gotten so used to it by now that I hadn't even realized how exhausting it's been to be the only one.

I glance at the clock in the kitchen to check the time. Good, I still have an hour to get ready for our date.

Date.

It's such a simple word, but to me, it holds so much meaning. Hunter is taking me on a *date.*

The thought makes me feel both giddy and nervous, to the point where my stomach has been twisted up in knots all day. I haven't even been able to eat, which is one of my favorite hobbies.

I shouldn't feel like this, considering it's just Hunter, but this is new for us. It makes everything so official. And it makes my crazy heart fall even more in love with him.

I just wish I knew if he feels the same way about me.

For me, I now know and admit I never really stopped loving him. He's the only one I've ever felt this way about, and as far as I can tell, he's the only one I'll ever love.

Now, I just need to know if he loves me too. If what he says about being all in is backed by love or just a desire to know his daughter.

I guess I'll know in time, right?

I mean taking that step is the only real way to know, no matter how terrifying it may be.

I make my way out of the kitchen and into the hallway, climb the stairs up to the second floor, and go to my room. I pull my phone out of my pocket and pull up the picture of a hairstyle Sabrina picked out for me tonight.

She said that since it was our first "real" date, I needed to look extra hot for Hunter. Never mind the fact that we have a child together and he's seen me at my worst.

I set my phone so that it won't lock on me and lay it against the mirror on my dresser. I pull out the curling iron, turn it on, and start to work my magic on my makeup.

I'm not much of a makeup artist. I spend too much time in the kitchen sweating to worry about what I look like, but for Sabrina's sake, I'm trying. Not only did she insist I need to look hot, but she's expecting pictures when I'm done.

I stare at the image of the model on my phone, trying to get the colors just right. Her eyes are smoky with some hints of blue and silver among the dark eyeshadow, her lips a glossy pink.

I copy what I see to the best of my ability, and I glance at myself in the mirror and frown. I completely messed up the smoky part of the eyeshadow. In fact, it looks exactly like what I do with it normally.

Oh well. I think I look hot, and honestly, that's all that matters.

As I start to work on my hair, my phone rings. I glance down to see London's name flash across the screen. I quickly release the curling iron and answer the Facetime.

Her bright blonde hair appears across the screen. "I already said no sweets. It's almost dinner time," she yells.

"I mean I wasn't planning on eating any sweets, but okay," I quip, flashing a big smile.

London jerks her head back to the phone and chuckles. "Sorry, Brayden decided he needed to raid the cookie jar just as I called you."

"Now, that's my kind of kid right there."

"I know, right? I always hate punishing him for things I do on a regular basis, but I mean I'm allowed to do what I want. He's not." London flips her hair and sticks her hand out with attitude.

I laugh, letting another curl fall loose around my head. "Me too, girl. The struggle is real as a parent."

"No doubt," London agrees, smiling eagerly. "So, are you ready for your big date?"

"What big date?"

"Oh, ya know, the one with that hot, hunky baby daddy of yours."

"Oh, right, that one," I joke, trying to play it cool and failing miserably. "I'm so nervous, but so excited at the same time."

We both laugh. One of the beauties about having friends with the same sense of humor and sass: you're always laughing.

"Speaking of your date, you gonna give it up tonight?" she asks, wiggling her eyebrows suggestively.

"What? Are we in high school again? Did I miss the flashback to the past?" I joke as my cheeks burn red.

London doesn't miss my blush. "Oh my God, you already did, didn't you?"

"Maybe," I respond with a smirk.

"Well, I'll be damned. Was it what you expected it to be?"

I shrug my shoulders, playing it cool. "It definitely didn't suck."

"Aw, I'm so jealous of you," London whines through the phone. "I haven't had sex in forever. I feel like I've forgotten how to do it."

"Trust me, you do not forget how to do it. I'm sure you'll get your fix soon."

London sighs and rests her head in her hand. "Doubt it. I'm too messed up with trust issues to let any guy near my body anytime soon."

"I get it, but you never know what might happen."

"Well, I do know that it will definitely not be my baby daddy wooing me off my feet, but I'm glad yours is, Ki. I'll let you get off here and finish getting ready, but I hope you have an amazing time."

"Thanks, girl, I'll talk to you soon."

I hang up and continue getting ready, letting my thoughts float around Hunter and all the time we've spent together lately. It's been wonderful, almost surreal at times, but the feeling of fear still sits somewhere in the back of my mind.

I force it away and remind myself that it's my life, and if I don't live it to the fullest, no one will.

When I finish my hair, I go to the closet and pull the teal lace sundress that Sabrina and I had decided on earlier out. The dress is cinched in at the waist to accentuate my curves and the skirt is just loose enough to leave some of my body to the imagination.

I slip into the dress and twist my arms around the back to zip it up and get it about halfway before the zipper snags on the fabric. With an annoyed sigh, I lean out the doorway of my bedroom and holler for my dad.

He grumbles about how hungry he is and how he just wants a damn snack as he stomps up the stairs. He finally peeks his head inside my doorway, his eyes confused as he asks, "What on earth are you all dressed up for?"

I roll my eyes. "I told you earlier this week. I'm going out to dinner with Hunter."

He shoots me a blank stare. "And you have to dress up for that?"

"Dad," I groan. "Can you just zip up my dress please?"

"Fine," he mutters as I turn my back towards him. He dutifully zips it up. When I turn back around, he gives me a gruff smile. "You look beautiful, Ki."

My dad doesn't compliment me often, but I love it when he does. "Thank you, daddy." I put a sweet kiss on his cheek.

He turns to leave, but stops halfway just to mumble, "Don't stay out all night this time."

"Not planning on it, Dad."

"Good, I'm too young to have two grandchildren."

I'm in agreement with him there. I love my baby girl, but I'm not ready for a second one just yet.

There are three restaurants in Sunrise, not including the café. First, you have the diner where you can find all things greasy and comforting. Second, you have the local bar, where you can pretty much find any bar food imaginable. Last, you have the fancy and expensive restaurant attached to the Grand Sun Hotel.

I don't know where I was expecting Hunter to take me for dinner, but I definitely was not expecting him to take me to the Amor, the restaurant attached to the hotel.

I wonder if Sabrina knew that's where he was taking me. It would definitely explain why she insisted I dress up for the date tonight.

Hunter pulls his truck into a space outside the restaurant entrance. I peer outside and get a glimpse of the inside of the restaurant, noting the dark lighting and red and brown tones throughout the room. The tables are lined with silverware, plates, and wine glasses.

I'm not gonna lie, I'm a little nervous. I've never eaten at a restaurant where there are three forks next to your plate.

When Hunter opens my door, I slide out of the passenger seat, a little more graceful this time thanks to the hand Hunter reaches out to me as I climb out of the truck. "I told you, you need me," he says with a smug look on his face.

"To get out of the truck? Yes. For everything else? No," I say, mimicking the way he's looking at me.

He chuckles. "If you say so. Come on, let's go eat." He guides me to the entrance with a hand on the small of my back.

I love when he does that. It makes me feel so safe and protected, it's almost like he's claiming me as his. As independent as I may be, I still enjoy that feeling.

The feeling that he wants me almost as much as I want him.

Hunter opens the door for me, and I glance at him with a quirk to my lips. "Pulling out all the stops tonight, aren't we?"

"Chivalry isn't dead yet," he quips.

He may just be right. I'm loving this side of Hunter. The side that acts like a gentleman.

I mean, what woman doesn't love that about a man. People think we want these caveman, alpha males, but really we just want someone to love us enough to pay attention.

Well, maybe some women want the strong, possessive male. But, not me.

I just want Hunter, the way he is now. Happy. Gruff. Strong and intimidating, but also loving. A family man. A gentleman. A man who lets me be independent and follows my lead.

Most of the time anyway. In the bedroom, I'm all for letting him call the shots.

We make our way up to the hostess stand. Hunter tells her the reservation information, and she leads us back to a table.

Once we're seated, I open the menu in front of me. The food looks so foreign to me. It's all fancy stuff, and I nearly balk at the prices.

I peer over my menu at Hunter who's studying the words in front of him intently. "You know, I would have been fine with a to-go burger from the diner and a ride in your truck," I say, referencing our go to activity in high school.

He looks up at me with the biggest grin that literally melts my cold, icy heart. "Yea, well, I thought you deserved a little more than that considering everything we've been through."

I can't argue with him there, but this place also isn't me. I've never been one for fancy restaurants and dressing up. I prefer my cheesy Southern Girl t-shirts, jeans, and a juicy burger or pizza.

"Hunter just you asking me on a date was enough. Literally, the date could have been dinner at my house, and it still would have meant so much to me."

"I'll keep that in mind for the next date." He winks at me as he stares back down at his menu.

Next date? All of this feels too good to be true.

And I can't help but wait for the other shoe to drop.

Thirty-Six

Hunter

I pull on the collar of my button up. It feels so stuffy in here, and this is definitely not my kind of place, but I chose this restaurant for Ki. I wanted to do something nice for her, to show her just how much she means to me.

But ever since she made the comment about my choice of place, I've been second guessing my decision. Should I have just gone with a diner date? Should I have taken her to the bar?

No, this date is supposed to be different from our normal routine of dinners at the house or the diner.

I shake the pointless worries from my thoughts. We're here now, and we are not leaving, so I'm going to drink my expensive whiskey and eat my $50 steak. And it better be the best damn steak I've ever eaten.

I glance up to look at Ki. She stares intently at the menu, her lips curved up into a sneer. "I really want to know how this restaurant manages to stay open in a town like this. I mean no one here can afford this place on a regular basis." Ki points to the menu as she mutters more about the prices, the same disgusted look still plastered on her face.

"I imagine the wealthy tourists have a lot to do with it," I point out.

"Smartass," Ki sticks her tongue out at me, and I smile like a damn fool.

I know I look ridiculous around her. I *feel* ridiculous around her, but she just makes me feel all kinds of shit.

Happiness, being the biggest one.

I never wanted a girl to have this much power over me, but I also hadn't realized just how amazing it could be either. Knowing that someone can make you laugh, cry, cuss, and love all at the same time.

Love. I've had a lot of time to think about it, and I'm certain that I love Ki.

She's it for me.

Case in point being the fact that I'm sitting inside a sophisticated and slightly intimidating restaurant all for her.

Or how my body reacted to hers the minute I saw her because, *damn,* does she look fucking gorgeous tonight.

But it's still not the right time to tell her I love her. When I do, it needs to be in a moment with no regrets, no discussion of the past, and no possibility that she'll think I'm saying it out of pity. Otherwise, it'll send *her* running this time.

Because after all this shit, Ki needs to know the love I feel for her is real.

The waiter steps up to the table, pulling me from my crazy, irrational thoughts. "Welcome to Amor, my name is Steve, and I'll be your waiter for this evening? May I start you out with a bottle of wine?"

A bottle? Hell no. I don't drink wine, and even if I did there's no way in hell I'd pay for a bottle of wine. The cheapest one started at $150.

"Go ahead, Ki, what would you like? Order whatever you want." But please, keep it under $20, I beg her with my eyes, really hoping she understands the telepathic message I'm trying to send.

"Can I get a glass of water and a glass of the Rosé?" she asks, crossing her arms on the pristine white tablecloth in front of her. She winks at me and mouths, "It's the cheapest one."

Thank God she'd heard my thoughts. "I'll have a whiskey." I say to the waiter.

"Any particular kind?" The waiter's lips straighten as he lifts his nose slightly up.

"Preferably the cheapest one you have," I smirk up at him.

He huffs out a breath just before he speaks. "I'll be right out with your drinks." He turns stiffly and heads to the back where a monitor sits. He taps furiously at the screen as he puts our drink orders in.

I focus my attention back on Ki. She places her head in her small, delicate hands and gazes at me, fluttering her eyelashes as she dazzles me with a smile.

She wants something from me. I can see it in her glimmering eyes. "What?" I ask.

"Would you kill me if I ordered the seafood platter? I'm really craving some lobster."

The seafood platter costs way more than my steak, but I also don't think I can turn down the face staring back at me. "Since you ordered the cheaper of the wines, I think I could *maybe* pass up killing you if you order the most expensive dish on the menu."

"Oh my, Hunter, what a gentleman you are!" she jokes with the thickest Southern accent she can manage. Her drawl is normally thick, but not that Southern Belle thick.

The waiter pops up next to our table again, this time glaring at Ki as she tries to hide her laughter. "Here are your drinks." He sets them down on the table, stiffens his back into a straight line again, and tilts his head up. "What can I get you to eat this evening?"

"I believe my lovely date will be having the seafood platter, and I would like the filet mignon, medium."

Take that pretentious jack ass.

There were two things I had missed when I was away for the last five years: my family (Ki included) and the sound of the waves hitting the beach. I'm not a surfer boy by any means but looking out over the ocean has always made me feel like anything is possible.

After dinner, Ki suggested we take a walk along the beach. We left the truck parked by the Amor and we set off down the path behind the hotel.

Now, we walk side by side as we step out onto the sand.

When we were younger, Ki and I would slip down to the ocean in the evenings and watch the darkness roll in over the waves. As we got older, we had this little spot under the boardwalk that we'd hang out in.

Most of the guys I went to college with talked about their field parties, but I talked about our beach parties. Although we had our fair share of field parties, too. It's the thing you do in a beach town, especially during the summer.

I stop to slip my dress shoes off and Ki does the same. With my shoes in one hand, I slip the other into Ki's hand.

It's been too long since Ki and I have done anything like this.

She gazes up at me, her face beaming with happiness. "Now, this is my kind of date," she whispers against the coastal breeze.

The smell of saltwater and seaweed instantly fills my nose. It sure is good to be home.

Ki and I walk hand in hand further out onto the beach until our feet feel the waves. "I hope I didn't totally ruin this night by taking you to Amor."

"This night is perfect, Hunter. Sure, the waiter was a snot, but dinner was amazing. I mean that seafood was so worth the $75 you paid for it." She looks up at me coyly.

"I'd do it all again just to spend time with you."

She stops walking just as a wave rolls over our feet. "You don't have to take me to fancy restaurants or on fancy trips to impress me. I've always been impressed by you."

Awkwardness takes over, and I'm not quite sure what to say. I tug on her hand as I start to move up the beach towards the boardwalk. "Remember when we used to come down here in high school?"

"Yea," she laughs. "If our parents knew what had gone on down here, they'd have rethought letting us hang out on Friday nights."

"You think they don't know what we did down here?"

She tilts her head to the right, thoughtfully. "You don't think they used to come down here when they were in high school, do you?" she asks as if she only just realized that our parents were teenagers once, too.

"Of course they did. In fact, I think I heard my dad talking to yours about it one time when we were younger."

She pouts her lips and crinkles her brow. "Hm, I guess I just always thought our parents were naïve about what happened down here."

"Honey, I think you're the naïve one."

She takes our connected hands and hits me with them. "Shut up, jerk."

"What happened to my usual nickname? I believe it's asshole?" I tease her.

She moves our hands back and forth as we make our way closer to the boardwalk. "I thought I'd try out a new one."

"I like asshole better."

"Fine, *asshole*." She quirks the corner of her lips up in a smile as we reach the wooden planks holding the boardwalk up within the waves.

She races ahead of me to the pole we used to claim as our own. "Hunter, it's still here," she shrieks a few feet away from me.

I inch closer to the pole and glance at the spot she points to with her finger: our initials. "I completely forgot we carved those down here."

"It was the first party of Senior year," she muses looking off into the ocean as it slowly turns to darkness. "You wanted to leave our mark on this place, so you decided to carve our initials. Of course, some alcohol may have been involved in that decision, but anyone who comes down here will forever wonder who they belong to."

As she continues to reminisce, I feel the sudden urge to spill my guts to her, to tell her that I love her. I just don't know if it's the right time yet.

What if she thinks I said them because I was caught up in the memories?

All I know is my heart is pounding, beating furiously in my chest. The feelings I have for Ki can't even compare to the year we won States in high school or even the National Championship in college. Nothing can compete with the way I feel in this moment.

I step closer to Ki and put one hand on her cheek and one on the back of her neck. Slowly I dip my head until our lips come together in a lust-induced inferno. I push my way inside her mouth, feeling the heat of the kiss intensify.

My body goes flush with her warmth against it. I need her just as badly as I needed her the other night.

I move away from her slowly, our mouths a few inches away from each other. "Truck? Now? Our spot?"

She knows what I'm asking. It's the place where Hannah was conceived. At first, she looks like she might say no, but I see a tiny sparkle of passion in her eyes. She nods her head and reaches for my hand.

Thirty-Seven
Makiya

I didn't stay out all night, but I also didn't come home until close to two in the morning.

And my dad knew it. He didn't say anything about it, but he also didn't seem thrilled about all the time I was spending with Hunter.

Almost two weeks have passed since our date, and we've been pretty much inseparable.

Everything about that night was perfect, and everything since has been even more so. We work together at the café during the day and sneak little kisses in the back office when Sabrina isn't looking.

He spends nearly every evening at the house with Hannah and me, helping me get her settled into bed and then having "us" time, as he calls it.

Over the last two weeks, I've started to feel like we're actually a couple. Besides the fact that we do everything together, we also find some pretty damn clever ways to make-out or do some even dirtier deeds.

That may very well be my favorite part. Well, that and watching him with Hannah.

A soft peck on my cheek pulls me out of my Hunter-filled thoughts.

Speak, or think, of the devil and there he stands next to me with a wide grin on his face. "Someone looks happy today." I say as I put my first round of pastries in the oven for the morning. "You're also here early," I note, catching the time on the wall as I turn back to him.

He grabs me around the waist and pulls me in tightly. His hands land just above the curve of my butt. "I wanted to catch some alone time with you this morning since Riley wants me to go out with him and the guys tonight."

I smirk up at him, mocking him with my eyes. "And what exactly does this *alone time* entail?"

Just as he leans into kiss me, the backdoor swings wide open. "Ew, gross," Sabrina squeals.

I peer around Hunter to see her standing just inside the kitchen with one hand covering her eyes. "Oh, stop it. We're not ten anymore."

"Kissing is gross," she whines, acting like we used to when we were kids.

I step out of Hunter's embrace, pick up the towel laying on the stainless-steel cooking table, and toss it at her. She catches it right before it hits her in the face. "Nice try, but I know you well enough to predict what you're going to do."

I roll my eyes and cross my arms. "Yea, right, okay."

"I knew you were going to do that, too," she insists.

Hunter just stands there next to me, laughing silently to himself. He waves between the two of us as he heads to the back office. "Carry on, girls."

Sabrina takes a few steps closer to me and puts one hand on each of my shoulders. "I'm really happy for you. I'm glad you've found a way back to each other."

I respond with a soft gagging noise as a wave of nausea tumbles through my body. *Oh my goodness, what is that smell?* I run straight to the employee bathroom and bring up what little bit I ate for breakfast.

"You okay?" Sabrina rushes after me, shutting the door behind her.

"Yea, I don't know what that was. Maybe I have a stomach bug or something," I say from where I crouch in front of the toilet.

Sabrina crosses her arms in front of her and lifts an eyebrow. "Yea, sure, or maybe you're pregnant," she smirks.

"I'm not pregnant," I scoff.

She peers down at me. "If you say so." Then, she turns and opens the door, leaving me alone and shaken up.

I couldn't be pregnant.

There's no way.

Besides, this is the first time I've been nauseous. It's probably just some kind of virus or something. I stand back up slowly, feeling a little better already. I haven't even had any other symptoms.

Nope. I'm not pregnant.

I'm.

Not.

Pregnant.

I slam the panini press down a little harder than necessary. I hate that my stupid stomach won't stop rolling like the ocean. And I hate that every single smell in this kitchen makes me want to throw up.

These damn stomach issues better be over soon. I know it's the stress of everything. It happens every time, but it's been almost two weeks. I just want to enjoy my job again.

I pop the press open again and pull out the nice, warm, and perfectly flattened ham and cheese sandwich. I place it on the plate, surrounding it with chips, just as Sabrina and London peak their heads into the kitchen.

Both of them eye me suspiciously with their hands behind their back like they're hiding something.

"What am I missing here?" I ask, slightly annoyed and completely confused.

"Is Hunter here?" London questions, darting her eyes around the kitchen as if she doesn't want to be seen.

I purse my lips and cross my arms in front of me. "Um, no, he left to run an errand. Why are you guys being so weird right now?"

Sabrina stands up straighter and London mimics her movement. "We have something we want to talk to you about, and we figured you probably didn't want anyone else to know." Sabrina says, sheepishly.

My two best friends walk towards me with their hands still tucked behind their backs. My heart begins to pump a little faster as they inch closer.

"You're really starting to freak me out," I state, urging my pulse to slow down.

When they reach the counter where I'm standing, they both lay a pharmacy bag on the table beside my wonderfully made sandwich.

"We think you're pregnant," Sabrina says simply.

London slaps her on the arm. "Could you really be any less sensitive about this?"

Sabrina glances at London. "What? It's the only reasonable explanation for the amount of time she spends throwing up and eating crackers throughout the day."

"It's not the only reasonable explanation." London rolls her eyes as she continues. "But it's definitely one explanation."

She looks at me, and I feel like a deer caught in the headlights of a bright red car zooming straight at me. "We think you need to take the tests just to be on the safe side. We know you don't want to think about the possibility, but Ki, you've been acting a lot stranger than usual."

I suck in a deep breath as the car hits me head on. I can't even argue with the two of them because I know they're right. No amount of denial is going to change the fact that I feel the same way I did five years ago.

And just like that...my missing period, worsening morning sickness, and five pregnancy tests have confirmed that I'm definitely pregnant.

I stare at the tests laid out on the bathroom counter. I should have waited until I got home to take them, but Sabrina and London were so darn insistent. I just wanted to get it over with to prove to them they were wrong.

And yet, I was wrong. How can this be? We used protection every time. Right?

I swore this was not going to happen again, but look at me, pregnant again.

And how am I going to tell Hunter? How is he going to react? Is he going to leave? Will this scare him off?

I mean one child is enough, but *two*. That's a lot to handle. Even I'm terrified.

Although my fear revolves more around Hunter than it does the baby.

I did it once and I can do it again, but I really don't want to raise this baby alone like the last time. I just don't know if I'll be the one to make that choice.

A knock sounds on the door. "Ki, you okay? You've been in there a long time," Hunter says from the other side.

Quickly, I grab the tests and toss them into the trash, covering them up with some paper towels. I brush my hair back out of my face and try to ease my nerves.

I can't tell him. Not yet.

My heart races and my hands shake as I open the door of the employee bathroom. "I'm fine, Hunter," I say as I close the door behind me.

I move through the kitchen and out to the front of the café, aware that Hunter is following me the whole way.

"Ki, you don't look okay," he continues. He reaches for my arm, and I shrug out of his grasp. He grimaces at the way I pull away from him.

I feel terrible, but I can't do this right now. The only reason I even took the tests at work is because Sabrina and London bought them and made me. I didn't even want to take them in the first place - mostly because I already knew what they would say.

Hunter continues to follow me as I step up behind Sabrina at the counter. She glances at me between customers, her face fraught with concern, jumping back and forth from Hunter to me.

She knows. I'm sure she can see the fear in my eyes. "Hunter, can you watch the register for me real quick? I need to talk to Ki."

He looks distressed, his face scrunched up in confusion, creating wrinkles around his eyes and on his forehead. He knows something is up, but at least he doesn't know what. Yet.

Sabrina drags me back to the office and shuts the door. "I have an idea of what those tests said, but please confirm for me."

One tear slides down my cheek, then another and another, until I can't keep the dam up any longer. Sabrina wraps her arms around me in a hug as I sob.

Every tear represents every fear I've ever had. They're taking over, making me want to curl up in my bed and ignore this entire disaster.

God, being afraid and constantly worrying really does suck the energy out of you.

Sabrina guides me over to the office chair and helps me sit down in it. "It's going to be okay, Ki. Hunter's here this time."

His name makes me cry harder. She remains silent, waiting for me to calm down.

After a few minutes, there are no more tears left to cry. "What if I tell him, and he decides to walk away? It's too soon, Sabrina. We've only just gotten back together. Things are really good between us."

Sabrina sits down on the floor in front of me, crossing her legs. "Look, maybe it is too soon, but it's happening. You can't keep this from him, not again. You're going to have to face your fears and tell him. And, if I'm right, I think you'll be pleasantly surprised at what happens."

"It's not that simple," I insist, whining slightly.

"Ki," she pauses to roll her eyes at me. "It *is* that simple. You're just scared. One day you're going to have to get over the fear of him leaving, or you're going to run him off yourself."

The words feel like a knife slicing through my heart. "You just don't understand," I yell in her face, standing quickly.

She jumps up just as fast. "Ki, go home. Clearly, you need to cool down and do some thinking," she grits out through clenched teeth.

I want to argue with her, but I can't. My heart is racing. My cheeks are flaming red. My fists are clenched tight by my side. I need to calm down, but I can't.

I'm so angry at myself for being so stupid. Again. You'd think that after the first time I'd be more careful. Obviously not.

I don't want to do this all alone again, but this thing with Hunter has always felt too good to be true. This is the shoe I've been waiting to drop.

Sabrina still stands in front of me, her own anger disappearing from her face. She puts a hand on each of my shoulders, centering me, bringing me back to reality. "Go home," she speaks slowly. "Hunter and I can handle the café. And you need to decide what you're going to do next."

I nod and grab my stuff from the table by the door. "Yea, okay."

I don't want to go home, but I don't want to stay here either. At least at home, Hunter isn't there.

Just as I begin to slip out the door, Sabina says, "Everything will be okay."

She may believe that, but I'm not so sure.

Thirty-Eight

Hunter

Sabrina steps up beside me at the register just as I finish serving the last guest in line. She leans her back against the counter and uses her hands as anchors on the top of it.

"Be honest with me. Is she okay?" I ask her even though I see the answer written in the frown on her face.

She shakes her head and taps her fingers on the edge of the counter. "No, she's not, but give her some space. Okay?"

"Space? Why does she need space?"

"She just needs to figure some things out."

"Okay, so where is she now?" I ask, my mind already freaking out. I'm obviously missing something big, but I have no idea what it could possibly be. Everything was fine yesterday, and now she needs to figure some things out?

"I told her to go home. I'd imagine you'll need to pick Hannah up from school." She pushes off the counter and starts back to the kitchen. "I'm going to get things prepped for tomorrow. Can you handle the front?"

"Yea, I got it."

Thankfully, today has been a particularly slow day which gives me time to try and figure out what the hell Ki needs space from.

I rack my brain, trying to come up with reasons or things she could possibly need to figure out. Does she not love me like I thought she did? Has she decided we aren't good together?

I'm going to drive myself mad if I keep doing this. I need to just listen to what Sabrina said. I'll give her some space \, and when I drop Hannah off later, I'll check on her.

For now, though, I follow the typical routine at the café. Normally, I don't work out front, but I've watched Ki do it enough to know what needs done. I clean the tables after people leave, gather orders, and make coffees until it's closing time.

When the clock hits two, I lock up the front door and head to the back. Sabrina is packing up the last bit of dough, and Mario is rinsing off the last few dishes from the day.

"Are you okay if I head out to pick up Hannah?" I ask Sabrina.

She brushes the flour from her hands and wipes them on a towel. "Yea, Mario and I can finish up here."

"Good, I'll see you tomorrow then." I turn to head to the office.

"Hey Hunter," she says so quickly that I almost don't understand her.

I shift sideways so I can see her. "Yea?"

"Promise me you won't leave her this time?" Her eyes frantically search mine, pleading.

"What?"

"Promise me you won't leave Ki. She needs you, Hunter, even if she thinks she doesn't. Not because she can't take care of herself, but because you're good for her."

"I'm not planning on leaving Sabrina."

"Yea, okay." She nods slowly.

I have no idea where this is coming from, but I brush off the uneasy feeling her words give me as I head into the office. Something is definitely going on, but I can't do anything about it until I figure out what it is.

I start to put away the files of receipts and invoices I was working on earlier, noticing a receipt that hadn't been in the business file this morning. Ki must have dropped it earlier. I pick it up to get a closer look.

The words pregnancy test flash through my mind as I read it printed five times on the receipt. "Sabrina," I yell through clenched teeth.

She rushes into the office, her face flushed. "What is it?"

I wave the receipt in front of her face. "She's pregnant, isn't she?"

Sabrina backs away from me slightly, her eyes darting between me and the wall behind me. "Hunter, I can't…"

"Don't even try to tell me you can't tell me," I cut her off before she can finish. "It's right here on the receipt. Is she even going to tell me about it?"

"Of course she's going to tell you. Why wouldn't she?"

I throw the receipt down on the desk in front of me and let out a guttural scream, rage pulsing through my blood. She knew when I went to the bathroom, and she didn't say anything.

Not a word.

How could she not tell me? *Again?*

I bawl my hands into fists and pound them on the desk in frustration.

She's pregnant. Again.

I'm going to be a father, and she didn't even tell me.

It feels like a knife slashes my gut as the realization hits me. She doesn't trust me enough to tell me. She's afraid I'll leave again; it has to be. What other reason would she possibly have *not* to tell me the second she suspected?

I pick the receipt up and stuff it in my pocket. Sabrina's still standing just inside the doorway. "I need to go," I growl as I stomp towards her.

She shifts to the side so I can pass around her. "Hunter," she calls behind me. "Be easy on her. She's scared."

I know she's scared, but I'm not going through this again. I'm not missing out on my child's life. I will *not* let her take that away from me for the second time. And I won't let her walk away from me again.

I pull my truck into Ki's driveway and shift the gear into park. The truck has barely stopped before I jump out the door and run up the porch steps.

Thankfully, I had the good sense to drop Hannah off at Mom and Dad's house before heading over here. Fuck knows I wouldn't want her to see me like this. It took everything in me not to emotionally explode after I picked her up from school.

I pound my angry fists on the door, getting louder and louder which each thud.

There's no answer.

"Ki, I know you're here. Open the door, please. We need to talk," I holler through the door, hoping she can hear me. I wait a few more minutes before I slam my fist against the door again.

She better answer the damn door. We need to talk about this. She's not going to keep me from this child. She doesn't get to make that choice this time.

I lift my arm to knock on the door one more time when I hear the lock click. The door swings open with enough fierceness that I expect to see an angry Ki glaring back at me, but my eyes meet her father's gruff face instead.

"I need to talk to Ki," I fire at him before he gets a chance to tell me to leave.

He keeps the door shut just enough that I can't see into the house around his large frame and grim face. "She doesn't want to see you right now."

Anger fuels the words that rush out of my mouth in a growl. "I don't care what she wants. I need to talk to her now."

He crosses his arms in front of him, making his stance firmer. His words come out harsh. "I think you need to leave now."

"I'm not leaving until she talks to me."

He leans his shoulder against the door frame. "This isn't about you right now, Hunter. This is about Ki, and she doesn't want to see you."

Is he for real? This isn't about me? This has *everything* to do with me. It's my child she's pregnant with. It's my child she doesn't want to tell me about. Of course this is about me!

"I know what this is about," I grit out through clenched teeth.

"Then, you should know that she needs some time alone to process everything," Mr. Carter says a little softer this time, sincerity in his voice.

His genuineness and the way the wrinkles around his eyes soften tell me he's just trying to protect his daughter. "I get that she needs to process the news. Shit, I'm processing it myself. But why does she need to do it alone? Why didn't she tell me herself?"

"I can't answer those questions for you, but I can ask you to think about this from her perspective. Remember that you left her last time, and she dealt with this alone."

"But she didn't have to. She made that choice for both of us. I'm not letting her do that again," I grumble in frustration.

I feel like all I do is repeat myself to Ki and to her father. Why can't they just believe me? I'm where I want to be, and as pissed as I am right now, I'm also really excited to be able to experience all the things I missed with Hannah.

Mr. Carter uncrosses his arms and places one hand on the door as if he's about to shut it. "Then, when she finally comes to you about being pregnant, tell her that."

That's it. That's all he says as he slams the door in my face and the lock clicks back into place.

No other words of wisdom. No timeframe for when Ki will finally talk to me.

Nothing.

Just a damn door in my face.

Slowly, I walk back over to my truck, contemplating everything that happened today, everything that's happened over the last few months. My life has changed so much.

When I came back, I had expected to start working with my dad, even though I never had the desire to work in construction. I had expected to live with my parents, be bored out of my mind, and maybe, by the grace of God, try again with Ki.

What I hadn't expected was to find out that I had a child that my parents and Ki managed to keep from me for five years. I never thought I'd end up being the family kind of guy or that Ki and I would make a second child together. Hell, I never thought she'd let me get close enough to even try.

Life has been a whirlwind since I got back, but it has made me realize I've always loved Ki. I never stopped loving her.

I don't know what would have happened five years ago if she'd told me about the baby or if I hadn't been such a dumbass. I'd like to think that I would have come home, been there for her, and maybe allowed myself to admit the truth about my feelings for her.

I'll never know for sure, but I do know what will happen this time. I know without a fraction of a doubt, it won't be anything like the last time.

Thirty-Nine
Makiya

There's a vigorous banging on the door booming through the house. I hear it clear as day from my room. I have an assumption as to who it is, but I'm not getting up from this bed.

I can't talk to him right now, and I'm hoping to God that Sabrina didn't tell him about the baby. But why else would he be here furiously pounding on the door?

"Makiya, it's Hunter. Are you going to come answer the door?" my dad hollers from the bottom of the stairs.

I knew I should have shut my door when I came up here. "No, I don't want to talk to him."

My dad stomps up the stairs and stops just inside my room, glaring at me. "I don't think he's going to stop until you do."

"Well, then he can keep pounding on the door if that's what he wants to do," I mumble as a I pull the plush blanket up around me, burrowing into its warmth.

"Why's he here, Ki? Better yet, why are you here? Shouldn't you be at work or picking Hannah up from school or something?"

"Remember the other night when you joked about not wanting another grandchild?" I pause, studying my father's face for a reaction, but there is none. His face remains stoic and firm. I wish I had his ability to mask my emotions.

He nods his head and backs up out of the room. I hear him stomp his way back down the stairs and unlock the door. I strain my ears, trying to listen to what they're saying, but all I can make out are mumbling sounds.

The door shuts again, and my dad clomps back up the stairs. He shuffles into my room and takes a seat at the desk by my bed. There's no sympathy on his face, no happiness or anger. Nothing.

The intensity of his gaze feels like daggers on my skin. "Explain. Now," he demands.

I sit there silently, fearful of my father and what he will say when I tell him the truth. I suck in a breath and let it back out. "I thought we were being careful."

"You thought?" he interrupts me abruptly, his voice booming louder than necessary and making me grateful Hannah isn't here for this.

"I mean we were careful, Dad. Just obviously not careful enough," I mumble, knowing the explanation is useless. I'm going to get a lecture either way.

"Ki, I thought you would be smarter this time, especially after Hannah. Why would you put yourself in this situation again? You have too much on your plate to add more to it."

His words pierce my heart. Doesn't he know I've thought about this a hundred times already?

How could I be so stupid?

How could I let this happen again?

I'm supposed to be wiser, but I got caught up in the magic of love and I made the same damn mistake again. I've been beating myself up over this for hours. The whole time I was worried about Hunter breaking my heart, but what if I'm the one who ends up doing it.

What if being stupid leads to Hunter walking out on me again? Won't I be the one to blame for it this time?

The sensible part of me keeps saying it won't be my fault. And I know my thoughts are completely irrational with absolutely no facts to back them up, but I can't help it.

I'm beyond scared and anxious. I've reached the level of fear where your thoughts no longer make sense and your body has gone into self-preservation mode.

I don't want to do it all alone this time. I want to do it with Hunter. I want him to be there for all the firsts. Not because I need him to be there, but because I'm in love with him, and I don't want to rely solely on myself anymore.

I want someone to lean on through the good and the bad.

My dad sits with me in silence. I can tell he's thinking about what to say to me next by the way his lips are twisted up in thought. "He knows," my dad finally blurts out.

My heart pounds harder and my hands begin to sweat. "What? How?"

"I don't know. He didn't tell me, but he does know. That's why he came today. He wants to hear it from you. He's desperate to know why you didn't tell him when you first found out."

"He is?" I'm confused.

How does he know? Sabrina wouldn't tell him. She's too protective of me. I hadn't spoken to him since the bathroom, and I sure as hell didn't mention it. Plus, I hid the tests. There's no way he would dig through the trash. That's just not Hunter.

Why would he be so desperate to know why I didn't tell him? Is it because he's mad at me for not telling him or because he wants to be part of the baby's life - a part of mine?

Now I feel *really* guilty.

The desk chair creaks as my dad moves around in it. "You need to tell him, Ki. He deserves to hear it from you, even if you're scared."

"I know, Dad. I know," I mutter as my finger traces lines in the blanket, avoiding my dad's gaze. I can't look at him. I don't want to see the disappointment in his eyes.

The chair creaks again as my dad stands. "If it's any consolation, I don't think he's going anywhere this time."

I glance up to see if my dad is serious, his eyes soft with a sliver of hope. "How do you know?"

"Because the man downstairs was furious that you didn't want to speak to him, insistent he needed to see you, and desperate enough to tell me he got my daughter pregnant."

My dad leaves the room, and I'm left with nothing but my irrational fears, a glimmer of hope, and an intense silence surrounding me.

Is my dad right about Hunter?

I don't know, and I'm too tired to find out right now. Maybe tomorrow.

My phone dings just as my eyelids begin to close. It's a text from Rose.

I'll keep Hannah here tonight. I hope everything is okay. Love you Ki.

My eyes fill with tears and my heart with despair. I really wish my mom were here right now to help me process everything, to tell me what to do. I need her wisdom now more than ever.

Forty

Hunter

I walk through the front hallway, following the soft sounds of laughter. Every ounce of anger melts from my body as I walk through the kitchen door and see Hannah standing next to my mom at the kitchen counter. She's covered in flour and what looks like cookie dough.

"Daddy," she squeals, struggling to climb down from the chair she's standing on.

A feeling of warmth washes over me, seeing my daughter with a bright smile on her face as she runs towards me. I bend down just in time to catch her tiny frame in my arms. "Hey there, princess."

She leans back, putting her hands on my face. "Are you sick like Mommy?" she asks, wrinkles of concern dampening her bright smile.

I glance up at my mother, looking for clarification. "Ki called me and said she wasn't feeling well," she says, apologetically shrugging her shoulders.

I turn back to Hannah and smile. "I'm okay."

Her smile grows wider. "Good, 'cause Gramma said I get to stay here tonight and it wouldn't be very cool if you were sick too."

"No, I suppose it wouldn't." I stand lifting her up with me. "So, what are we making tonight?"

"My favorite cookies, duh," Hannah says like I should know what they are.

I take a peek into the bowl, noting the chocolate chips peeking out of the cookie dough. "Let me guess, chocolate chip cookies?"

"Yes," she yells excitedly as I place her back down onto the chair next to my mom.

"Can I help?" I ask, reaching in to grab some extra cookie dough off the side of the bowl.

Before I even get my hand back out of the bowl, Hannah slaps me. "No, not if you're going to eat the dough."

"Why can't I eat the dough?"

"Because Gramma says it could have Samanella in it, and if you eat the dough now, there won't be enough to make all the cookies," Hannah states with her hands on her hips, looking so much like Ki.

I brush the cookie dough off my finger. "Fine, I won't eat the cookie dough, but these better be some really good cookies."

"Of course, they are. They're Gramma's famous recipe."

I snort out a laugh, and my mom slaps me across the back of the head. She puts her finger to her lips shushing me. Guess that means she doesn't want me to spoil the beans – her famous recipe is actually the recipe on the back of the chocolate chip bag.

"Okay, let's finish this. What do we need to do next?"

For the next hour, I follow the instructions of Hannah. She tells me how big the cookies should be, when to take them out of the oven, and where to put them once they've cooled down. If she doesn't end up the president of something one day, I'll be shocked because damn if she isn't a bossy little thing.

But I love every minute of it because it gives me more time to get to know this tiny angel that I somehow managed to help make. Not to mention she's the only thing keeping me sane right now.

I wish Ki could see this, see how much I love this and want this.

When all the cookies are baked and stored in their proper cookie containers, I take Hannah upstairs, get her in the bath, and set for bed. She looks up at me with familiar eyes. "Daddy?" she says more as a question than a statement.

"Yea, princess," I say, pulling her into my side as I climb onto the bed next to her.

"I'm glad you came back for me."

Those words pierce me to my core, and I can't help but let the wave of sadness and regret wash over me. "Me too," I whisper, choking back the tears.

I'm not a man who cries, especially not in front of his daughter, but I'm not sure I can hold it in much longer – all my mistakes are threatening to tear down the fortress of protection I've built.

"Mommy told me you left because you weren't ready to be a daddy, but I think you're the best daddy in the whole world," she says softly, laying her tiny hand on my chest.

And that's it. Those words are my undoing. The tears fall silently down my cheeks, and I try so damn hard to hide them from Hannah.

"And I'm really glad you get to be my daddy." She keeps speaking as if I'm not losing my ever-loving mind over here.

"You know, princess, I'm really glad I get to be your daddy, too."

"I love you," she whispers, snuggling deeper into my side and closing her eyes.

"I love you more," I say in between the tears, and I've never meant those words more.

I never knew I could love someone as much as I love this precious angel beside me. I don't know what I did to deserve someone so perfect, but I'll be damned if I ever mess this up again.

I make my way back downstairs once I've wiped up all my tears. Hannah has been with me a million times over the last few weeks, but that's the first time she's said those words – the very same words I've been dying to tell Ki.

I don't know what I'm doing anymore. I'm so far out of my element. I mean I'm bawling my eyes out like a baby over some simple words my daughter said.

I turn the corner into the living room and hear the muffled sounds of my mother and brother talking.

Mom looks up just as I round the corner. "There you are. Did Hannah go to sleep all right?"

I nod, hoping the red around my eyes isn't too noticeable. The last thing I want is an inquisition by my mom.

She just smiles and stands. "Well, I think I'm going to head to bed, too. Your dad should be home soon, just tell him his dinner's in the microwave," she says, placing a kiss on my cheek before walking out.

No matter how old I get some things never change.

I look at my brother, sitting down in the armchair across from him. "Got a big project going on?" I ask, knowing it's the only reason my dad wouldn't make it home in time for dinner.

"Yea, someone paying big bucks for us to build a mansion of a house down on the beach, but they gave us a crazy ass deadline. Dad's trying to alternate the workers each night, so we all aren't working late every time."

"Makes sense," I say.

Silence falls between us as I decide whether I want to talk to Riley about my shitshow of a life or not.

I soak in the silence, letting it drown out every insane emotion and crazy doubt floating through my mind.

The silence doesn't last long though, and it doesn't surprise me. Riley's never been one for silence.

"So, I hear you've got some shit going on right now," he says nonchalantly.

"You could say that," I grunt. I'm really not sure I want to talk about this, but I know he won't let it go.

Riley leans his arms on his knees. "Wanna talk about it?"

"Would it make a difference if I said no?"

"Nope," he says.

I chuckle. I guess that's one of the fun things about having Riley for a sibling. He just can't let things go, and he always wants to talk.

"You know talking about things helps?"

"So, what, you're a shrink now?"

"No," Riley chuckles, "but that would be some fun shit. Could you imagine me listening to people drone on about all their problems all day long?"

I laugh at the thought, mostly because Riley can't go an entire conversation without making some kind of smart-ass remark.

Even if he'd be a shit therapist, he's not wrong. Maybe I would feel better if I talked about it.

I sigh, finally giving in. "I'm pretty sure Ki is pregnant, but I can't say for sure because she won't fucking talk to me and I have no clue what to do about it."

"Have you tried going to see her?" Riley asks.

"Of course, I've tried to see her. She won't come to the door. She won't answer my calls or texts." I growl in frustration. I mean what more can I do.

I lean back in the chair, closing my eyes.

"Maybe she just needs some time," he suggests, and I cringe.

Time. I've heard that word so many damn times in the last few days. I'm sure she does need time, but what about me? Don't I count in this matter?

"Look, Hunter, don't take this the wrong way, but it's kind of like history is repeating itself. Can you blame her for being a little confused and scared about all this?" Riley asks, concern wrinkling his face.

I know my brother's right, but it still doesn't make anything about this easy. I want nothing more than to go to Ki, to enjoy this moment with her because that's what we should be doing. We should be celebrating this together as a family.

Instead, she's doing God knows what, all alone, refusing to leave her damn house, and I'm here talking it out with my brother. Everything about this is so fucking messed up.

"No, I can't blame her," I groan, hating that my brother's right and also hating the fact that I know I have no choice but to wait this whole shit fest out.

Riley stands to leave, his large frame staring down at me. "It also wouldn't hurt to lay it all on the line."

I crinkle my brows. "What do you mean?"

"Tell her the truth. Tell her how you really feel. I bet that's the real reason she's not talking to you," he states before walking out of the room.

I don't know why that hadn't occurred to me before, but it sure makes a hell of a lot more sense now. How can she possibly know how I feel – how this makes me feel – and what I want if I haven't told her yet?

Forty-One
Makiya

I walk through the local cemetery, heading straight to the large oak tree that marks the spot where my momma's gravestone lies. The sun is barely awake and the soft sounds of birds chirping fill the air around me.

I have no idea why I'm here at the ass crack of dawn, but sleep evaded me all night and I just needed my mom.

I come to a stop just in front of the large marble engraved with *Loving Wife and Mother*. It's not the same as seeing her in person, but at least I feel a little closer to her here.

I lean down into the dewy grass, not caring if my pants get wet or not. No one is going to see me here anyway, and if they do, what do I care? My life's a shit fest at the moment.

I brush some branches off the marble and sit back. "Hey, Mom," I whisper, feeling completely stupid but also needing this so much. "I know I haven't visited in a while. Life's been kind of crazy lately."

That's the understatement of the year.

"But I know you'd be happy about everything going on." I pause, needing a moment to organize my thoughts.

I feel so silly sitting here talking to a large stone and worrying about how to tell it that Hunter is back, but I can't help it. Maybe it's the sheer fact that I know I won't be able to talk about him without expressing my deepest darkest feelings for him. Or maybe it's simply the fact that I'm talking to nothing that's making me pause to organize my thoughts.

Gah, I'm a mess – a big freaking mess. What is wrong with me?

I take a deep breath and brush my fingers over the engraving on the stone. A tear slides down my cheek, followed by another and another until I can't control them anymore.

"I wish you were here, Mom. I need you so much right now. I know I still have Dad, but it's not the same," I say, wiping the tears that have made it to my chin already.

I suck in another deep breath, trying to calm my breathing and convince myself to just let it all out.

"Okay, here goes nothing. So, Hunter's back. He showed up a while ago, saying he came back for his brother's wedding. I'm a little skeptical about the truth of that since his first stop was to see me, but who knows?

"Anyway, he found out about Hannah and said he wanted to know her and be a part of her life, which he's done. I wish you could see Hannah with him, Mom. It's almost like he's always been a part of her life. She's so happy he's here."

Hell, I'm happy he's here, too, but saying that out loud is too much for me to handle right now. I mean I've barely processed my feelings about him. Sure, I know how I feel, admitting my feelings about it right now just isn't possible for me.

It makes it too damn real.

And I am so not ready for real.

Yea, but you're pregnant with his child. You kind of don't have a choice but to face reality here, I remind myself as if I hadn't thought about it a million times in the last few days.

I sigh, cutting my thoughts off and staring at my mom's name engraved in fancy script.

"I'm pregnant," I blurt out. "And I'm terrified to tell Hunter. I don't know why because he's proven me wrong so many times already, but I can't help the sick feeling that two kids might be too much for him.

"Hell, two kids are too much for *me* at the moment, and I've had five years of being a mom. Hunter has only had a few weeks of being a dad. And if I feel that way, why wouldn't he feel it ten times more?" I ramble on, letting all my thoughts and worries pour out.

"But what if he is okay with it? What if he's excited for it? What if this whole pregnancy doesn't turn everything upside down but makes it all right again? I just don't know what to do," I cry, fresh tears sliding down my face.

A soft breeze washes over me, and its warmth feels like a hug, wrapping me up and squeezing me tight. I picture my mom's arms around me and her voice telling me it will all be okay.

And for the first time since she passed, it almost feels like she's here with me, like I can feel her spirit riding on the breeze. It sounds completely insane, but it comforts me.

I embrace the feeling and let my body relax into it. Soft words float across my mind as if my mom is speaking to me, "*You don't need me to tell you what to do. You already know what you need to do. You just need to find the courage first and trust that things will work out the way they should.*"

More tears soak my cheeks. I do know what I need to do. I need to tell him. I just don't know if I can find the courage to do it.

I suck in a deep breath and stand up slowly. "I miss you more and more every day. I love you so much, Mama. I'll see you later."

I turn and head back towards my car. I could sit there all day crying and whining, but it isn't going to change things.

I climb into the driver's side of my car and just sit there, breathing in and out deeply and trying to relax my muscles.

I just can't believe it. I can't believe I'm going through this again. I just really, desperately hope it doesn't turn out like last time.

Because I'm in way too deep.

So deep that I don't think I can come back from it this time around.

Forty-Two

Hunter

It's been two weeks since Ki ran out of the café, I found out she's pregnant, and her dad told me to let her process everything.

Two weeks.

I haven't called her.

I haven't texted her.

Okay, maybe that isn't entirely true, but I've tried not to contact her. Much.

I've been giving her space. She hasn't shown up to the café. She had asked Sabrina to run things for a bit, which kind of disappointed me when Sabrina told me.

After all the things I've been doing for her here, I'd have thought she'd ask me to watch things. I've worked my ass off here for her over the last few weeks. I know the business side of things far better than Sabrina does.

Although the fact she's not currently speaking to me probably has a lot to do with the decision.

I just keep trying to remind myself that Ki will come to me when she's ready. I just wish I knew when that will be. I'm starting to think it will be never, considering the radio silence I'm receiving from her.

And, if I'm being completely honest, the whole giving her space thing pisses me off. She's acting like she's the only one processing this news or involved in the whole thing. She's being completely self-centered, locking herself away in her house and deciding when it's right for me to know.

She should have told me the minute she found out. I think that's what pisses me off the most. She made the damn decision for me again.

I get that she had to do it alone the first time, but I'm here this time. Hell, I was there when she took the damn tests, yet she's still deciding for me.

That's it.

I'm not waiting any longer. This is bullshit.

I gather up my stuff from the office in the café. I don't even tell Sabrina I'm leaving.

I drive straight to Ki's house, where I know she's been holed up the last few weeks, avoiding me. Her dad's truck isn't here which is a good thing. If I'm persistent enough, she'll have to answer the door this time.

I run up to the door. I barely get the chance to knock before Ki opens it. She doesn't say anything, just motions with her hand for me to come in.

"How did you know I was here?" I ask as I step into the house. She motions for me to follow her into the living room.

"I'm psychic," she replies sarcastically.

I sit on the couch, and she sits in her dad's recliner across from me. "Seriously, Ki? How did you know?"

She tucks her feet up under her bottom and pulls her knees to her in a fetal position. "Sabrina called and told me you'd disappeared. And then I heard your truck in the driveway. Is it really necessary for it to be so damn loud?"

"Yea, it's how people know I've arrived somewhere," I tease. She doesn't look amused though. In fact, she looks exhausted. Dark circles lay under her eyes, and her lids droop a bit.

She stares at the wall behind me, silence filling the room. I have no idea what to say. I want to be angry and mad. I want to yell and accuse her of all sorts of things, but I can't. She looks lifeless, weak, and so vulnerable sitting across from me. Maybe this whole thing wasn't a good idea.

313

"I'm sorry I didn't tell you," she says meekly, pulling her legs closer to her chest.

"Why didn't you?"

"Because I couldn't believe this shit happened again. It's like where you and I are concerned we can't seem to remember the whole protection thing. And I was angry at myself for being so stupid again."

I bend forward, resting my elbows on my thighs and clasping my hands together, my gaze never leaving her face. "It takes two to make a baby, Ki. We both were stupid about it, but it happened. It's no one's fault."

A tear slides down her cheek. "I know, but things were going so well between us. Now that, I'm pregnant, I didn't know how you'd react. If you'd be happy or pissed. If you'd run or stay. All those unknowns…they scare the hell out of me."

I want to go to her, to hold her and show her that I'm not leaving, but I don't, not yet. "Were you going to tell me about the baby?"

"Yea, I just needed some time to think first. It was such a surprise to me." She pauses, tilting her head a bit and scrunching her pert nose up. "How did you find out?"

"I found the receipt from the tests when I was cleaning up that afternoon. Then, Sabrina confirmed it for me. Although I don't understand why you told her and not me?"

I should have been the first to know. Yet, I wasn't. It's like Ki wants to keep these secrets from me, like she doesn't really want me to be part of her life.

I hope I'm wrong about that because I want to be part of her life more than anything, especially now. I'm not missing my second child grow up.

Even if Ki doesn't want me to be part of her life, I'm still going to be here. I love her, and I love this baby more than I ever thought I could.

At first, the shock was stronger, but the more time I had to think about it, the more excited I became. I'm more than ready this time to be a father.

She breaks the silence that persists between us with a soft huff of air from her thin, heart-shaped lips. "She bought the tests for me. She's the one who thought I was pregnant, but when I missed that time of month, I figured I'd better check to make sure. I didn't know she'd gone the day before and bought some. She gave them to me that morning and told me to take them."

"I see." I don't know what else to say to her, so I leave it at that.

It's her move now.

She sets her feet down on the floor and bends forward, resting her arms on her thighs, almost mimicking my stature. "Do you want this baby?" Her eyes don't meet mine. Instead, they rove across the bland, beige carpeted floor.

"Yes, of course I do." I stand and make my way to her. I kneel down in front of her, forcing her to look me in the face. I need her to see the truth that seeps from my eyes.

"Are you sure?" Her lips shiver with worry and tears fill the corners of her eyes.

"I've never been surer, Ki. There's nothing I want more than you and this baby." I place my hands on top of hers and squeeze gently.

I hope she sees the truth in my eyes. I'm angry that she didn't come to me first. I'm pissed that she didn't think all this through with me, but I love her more than life itself. I want this.

All of this.

With her.

She doesn't know that yet, but she will.

Forty-Three

Makiya

My mind swirls with a million thoughts.

Does he really mean that?

He hasn't said he loves me, which is what I desperately want to hear, but he said he wants the baby and me.

So that's a good thing, right?

I stay silent as I continue to process what he said.

My heart longs to hear those three simple words that would make all this fear and worry scamper away faster than a raccoon running from a hound.

Honestly, I can't blame if he doesn't want to say them to me. I haven't exactly been the best at letting him into my heart again.

I keep pushing him away.

It's what I do best.

Push people away.

I don't want to take any chances that might hurt me in the end, but how much longer can I live like this?

Constantly pushing people away. Living a lonely existence with just my dad and Hannah.

Is that the life I really want?

I mean I've tested Hunter, time and time again. He's proven to me that he's sticking around this time.

Hell, I haven't spoken to him in days. I didn't even tell him about the baby.

Yet, he's here in my living room.

If he doesn't mean what he says, why'd he come back a second time?

"Do you really mean that?" I ask as the warmth of his hands on mine eases my mind.

"Yes, I mean it."

"Because babies are hard. They keep you awake all night. They cry and cry and cry some more, and you never really know what they need. They want constant attention, and it's going to be a major adjustment." I ramble on and on, trying, in some twisted way, to convince him that he doesn't really want this.

It's my sick need to test his virtue.

He drops his hands to the side and stands, clenching his fingers into angry fists. "Damn it, Ki, why won't you just believe me? Why do you keep pushing me away?"

I stand in front of him. My own anger pulsing through my veins. He doesn't know. How can he possibly not know?

"Because I'm in love with you, you jackass, and I'm terrified that you're going to leave when things get hard just like you did before," I blurt out in frustration and cover my mouth as my eyes grow wide.

Shit, did I just confess that? For real, and not under the guise of sex this time.

"You what?" He asks, his eyes round with emotion.

"You heard me!" I yell, taking my hands away from my face.

I don't know why I'm so angry, but it's like he lit a fire under my ass, and I can't put it out now.

His brows crinkle together, the wrinkles on his forehead becoming more pronounced. "Yea, I did, but I wasn't sure I heard you correctly." His lips lift into a cocky smirk. "Mind saying it again, without the jackass at the end?"

I'm definitely not saying it again now that he's being a cocky asshole.

I stomp my foot and spin on my heels, but his hand catches my wrist. He spins me back into his arms, and my face collides with his firm chest.

"I'm in love with you too, Ki," he whispers as he drops his lips to mine.

I don't have time to process what's happening. His lips find mine in an angry collision filled with electrifying hunger. Him finally telling me that he loves me makes this kiss so much better.

Our lips break apart long enough for Hunter to ask, "Is your dad coming home today?"

"Not until late tonight," I say breathing heavily.

"Good, I need you now." He points to the stairs and I know exactly what he's thinking.

My mind is way ahead of him. I grab his hand and lead him up the stairs.

It's still fairly dark when I wake, with a thin line of light where the sun is just beginning to peek over the ocean.

Hunter lays beside me. His chest moves up and down with soft breaths.

Last night was better than I could have ever imagined. Not only did Hunter say he loved me, but he made love to me like he never had before.

For the first time, I felt deep in my soul that he meant the words he'd been saying for over a month now.

Even now, as I lay next to him watching him sleep peacefully, I still feel it: the love he has for me, the knowledge that he won't leave.

I can't promise I won't try to push him away again. I can't change the stubborn and cautiously strong side of me. It's become a part of what makes me the sassy, independent woman I am.

However, I *can* promise that I'll remind myself of this moment, this feeling, anytime I get scared and think of pushing him away.

The yellow orange of the sun begins to peak through the windows in my bedroom. I nudge Hunter to wake him up.

He grumbles a bit, and I give him a soft kiss on the lips. "Wake up," I whisper.

His eyes open, just barely. "What?" he mumbles in sleepiness.

He's not a morning person, but today he will be. "I want you to come watch the sunrise with me. Please?" I say the last word with a slight whine to my voice.

He groans as he pushes himself up in the bed. He gives me a soft kiss, then reaches for his shirt that lays on the nightstand.

We slip out the window in my bedroom and sit on the roof that hangs over the east side of the house.

Hunter pulls me into his side, and I lean into his warmth. "I love you."

"I love you too." I stare out at the sun, slowly making its way into the world and out of the darkness for a new day, a new beginning.

"I'm so happy, Ki. I've never been happier, and I can't wait to keep living this life with you, to see our baby, and to watch Hannah grow. I didn't know what I was missing until I found you again. Now, I can't imagine this life without you two. Well, three now." I laugh.

He has no clue how much I need to hear those words. "I'm so happy, too. I never thought we'd find our way back to each other, but I'm so glad we did. If I'm being honest, I've been in love with you since we were kids. I never stopped loving you, even when I thought you weren't coming back."

I hear his heart beating softly in his chest, and I know I'm home, with him by my side.

"Here's to our future, to our fresh start," he says as his lips meet mine. They fumble for a second as his body wakes up, but once it does, the heat and the passion lead his movements.

Our lips fit together, moving in a perfect symphony of love and happiness.

And that's it.

The end.

Just kidding.

It's nowhere near the end. It's just beginning, like the sunrise we sit in front of together right now. Hunter and I found our way back to each other.

Our love.

A Sunrise Kind of Love.

You know?

The one with new beginnings.

Acknowledgements

I don't know why writing this page is always so hard for me because I'm constantly saying thank you to everyone for everything. But for some reason, I can't seem to decide whom I should thank first. So, in no particular order, here it goes!

First and foremost, thank you to my family. You all are the reason I have the strength and the courage to fight for my dreams, to make every single one of them come true. For the longest time, I felt unlovable and completely broken, but you're always there to remind me that I'm worthy of all the love and gifts this world has to offer.

Thank you to my wonderful and talented husband. Not only have you supported me on this journey in every way possible, but you've also covered all my design and layout needs. You are truly a blessing, and our love inspires my stories every day.

Thank you to the absolutely amazing Bethany Hendrix for taking time out of her busy schedule to edit and answer all my pain in the butt questions.

Also, I need to send a shoutout to the incredible Nouna Anthony for redesigning my website and my marketing plan and always believing in my writing, even though she hates reading romance novels.

Of course, I can't forget the wonderful writers, friends, and bloggers that I've met along this journey. You truly are the most amazing and supportive people. I've loved every minute of getting to know you all, and I can't express how much I appreciate you letting me bombard you with questions and promos. Thank you all so much!

And, I desperately need to thank my readers. None of this would be possible without you and your encouragement. I'm beyond grateful for all of you.

Last but not least, I want to thank the good Lord above for giving me the strength I need to keep going each day. My life has not once been easy, but I know I'll make it through.

About the Author

Loran Adelle Davis writes sweet, contemporary romance stories with strong, sassy Southern women as her main characters, and don't let the "sweet" fool you!

She found her love for reading and writing strong female leads while completing her Bachelor's in English at a small Appalachian College. She furthered her craft of writing through her English degree and learned a lot about the stories she wanted to tell the world. With the help of her mentor, the Chair of the English Department, she determined that she would do what she loves – writing.

Currently, she resides in South Carolina. She works on her writing and her business LA Davis Books, LLC in the mornings and teaches toddlers in the afternoon. Her love for children and writing hold equal places in her heart. When she isn't writing or working, she enjoys traveling, trying new foods, reading, spending time with her family, and watching Hallmark movies.

Find Me On...

Facebook: www.facebook.com/ladavisbooks

www.facebook.com/loranadelledavis

https://www.facebook.com/groups/loransbooklovers

Instagram: www.instagram.com/loranadelledavis

Twitter: https://twitter.com/LoranDavis

Or Visit My Website

Website: www.ladavisbooks.com

Don't forget to sign up for my newsletter or join my Facebook Reader Group for special updates!

www.ingramcontent.com/pod-product-compliance
Lightning Source LLC
Chambersburg PA
CBHW060519180626
46817CB00002B/419

* 9 7 8 0 9 9 8 7 9 5 6 6 9 *